not so thanks in advance

WARTS & CLAWS INC SERIES (BOOK 3)

CLIO EVANS

"And I knew exactly what to do. But in a much more real sense, I had no idea what to do." — Michael Scott, The Office

warning!

HR Department:

Dear Reader,
There have been Reports of the following in
this office: CNC, primal play, tentacles,
virgin monsters, copy room fucking,
breeding without pregnancy, chasing,
filming during sex and sending video,
double penetration, mating bites, omega
heats and more.

If any of this makes you uncomfortable,
please report it to your HR rep
immediately.

Not So Thanks in Advance—
Warts & Claws Horn-y Resources

CHAPTER ONE
it's not stalking

BILLY

NO TYPICAL OFFICE-WORKING demon in their right mind would be waiting in the parking garage an hour early so that they could watch their crush drive in.

But I wasn't in my right mind.

It had been two weeks since more chaos had occurred in my workplace. In the first round, I was able to avoid most of the damage. But the second, I ended up being kidnapped by an ex-employee and then escaped with my HR agent.

At least my HR agent was friendly, but still.

It was a hellish environment to work in, but I liked hell. I was a demon, after all. A monster. A creature that craved a little chaos in the morning with my eggs and toast.

From what I had gathered, there was a group of individuals working to kidnap omega witches. I wasn't sure what entirely for, but... I'd been around long enough to know how powerful they could be.

But there had never been this many of them, goddamn it.

Last week, Alex brought in some of the witches that had escaped the evil enemy's hands. He had given them a job at the office to help them get back on their feet. Some of them seemed to be okay, and some of them not so much. But, overall, there was one problem— one of them was mine.

Or they *would* be mine.

If they noticed me.

The omega witches always came in early and left early. Sometime over the weekend, I decided that I would have to take matters into my own hands.

What better way to start my campaign of getting in Jaehan's pants than to begin on a Monday.

I watched as headlights flashed across the concrete, a silver hatchback pulling in. It pulled into a parking spot behind me, making me smile.

It was go-time.

I started to get out of my car, grabbing my bag and coffee mug. I shut the door just as he did, drawing his attention over to me.

Jaehan was too sexy for his own good. He always wore a crisp button-down and dark slacks with a leather belt and shoes, his black hair always damp in the mornings. He had warm beige skin, deep brown eyes, and a smooth face that I wanted to hold between my claws.

He gave me a sleepy smile, turning to head for the elevators.

I followed him, giving him just enough space so he wouldn't think I was stalking him.

Not stalking, I reminded myself. It wasn't stalking. Just making sure our paths crossed.

Besides, was it really stalking if he was meant to be mine?

The two of us walked across the garage, meeting at the elevator. Jaehan pressed the button, waiting patiently for the doors to slide open.

"Good morning," I said.

"Morning," he chuckled. "You're here early."

Did that mean he had noticed me before?

Not that I wasn't noticeable. In my office form, I looked like a human, but with six eyes, pointed fangs, and fingers that ended in claws. I often wore nicer shirts with pants, my black hair falling in curls down to my neck, and occasionally my form would turn a little more demonic.

Especially if darkness touched me.

Once in the dark, I could not stay in my human-passing form. Once shadows washed over my body, they warped me into my preferred form. A demon with the lower half of a black-furred satyr, and an upper half made of darkness. Still with six eyes, claws, fangs, and even black wings that sprouted from my spine.

In both of my forms, my cocks were the same. I couldn't hide either one of them.

Still, I wasn't the most noticeable demon.

"Yeah, I offered to come in and work overtime," I said easily.

"I thought Inferna forbade overtime with the threat of being tossed out the window from the ninth floor?" Jaehan asked, a little grin tugging at his lips.

The doors slid open, and he stepped in. I followed him, my heart pounding. "Well, sometimes there are exceptions."

Jaehan was about to respond when a dark tentacle slid through the doors, separating them before they could shut.

Damn it. I had really believed I would have Jaehan alone for a few moments.

I arched a brow, taking a step back for the monster. I had never seen him before, and his appearance was one I couldn't help but look over twice.

He was tall, even taller than me. His skin reminded me of opal, a shining white with glints of different colors. He had long white hair and so many tentacles, each of them an ombre color.

He was...stunning.

He was also shirtless.

"Uh," Jaehan cleared his throat. "I have an extra shirt if you need one, friend."

The creature froze, his back stiffening. He turned around, looking at Jaehan.

"*What?*" he snarled, his eyes wide.

A low growl left me, a soft warning.

His head swiveled, his eyes meeting mine. "What? Both of you can see me?"

"Yes?" Jaehan and I both said.

His lips parted, his cheeks turning bright pink. "What the fuck?"

"What do you mean what the fuck?" I asked. "Why the fuck are you coming to work shirtless?"

"Because I'm fucking invisible," he said, staring at me like I was a ghost.

"You're not," Jaehan said. "In fact, you are very, very visible. Inferna will lose her shit on you if you come to work without a shirt on."

"No one can see me," he said, gesturing at his very massive and visible body.

I gave Jaehan a side-look. This guy was obviously having problems.

"No one will see me," he said. "I'm invisible. I'm a ghost."

"You're not," I said, crossing my arms. "Did you eat mushrooms or something?"

"No!" he exclaimed.

"Hey, it's okay," Jaehan said softly. His scent became stronger, a wave of calmness rushing over me.

Followed by a wave of hunger.

What the fuck?

"What's your name?" Jaehan asked.

"Charlie," he answered, shaking his head. "This is impossible. That the two of you can see me."

I looked at Jaehan again, and there was a silent agreement. We would let Art or Inferna know that someone was cracked out, and they could take it from there.

Charlie shook his head again and turned, hitting our floor button with one of his tentacles. He kept muttering to himself.

Jaehan let out a small breath, his scent spiking again.

"Fuck," I mumbled.

His scent. It was enough to make me growl. I could feel my cocks hardening, a lustful hunger rising up.

"For fuck's sake," Charlie said, turning to look at Jaehan. "Are you in heat?"

Jaehan made a noise, backing into the corner of the elevator. "I'm not. Sorry, I don't know what's happening."

I growled, glaring at Charlie. I was about to pop off on him, but the elevator doors slid open.

Charlie turned, leaving the elevator immediately.

"What the fuck?" Jaehan whispered, panting softly. "Fuck."

"Are you okay?" I asked, but I held my breath.

Jaehan made a face. "I don't know what's happening."

"You smell like you're in heat," I said, my voice softening.

Jaehan shook his head and then pushed past me, leaving me alone.

Fuck. I'd scared him off. And why wouldn't he be scared? He was an omega witch who had escaped the evil bastards and had just been in the elevator with two monsters who wanted to devour him.

I sighed and stepped out into the hall, walking through the office and straight to Art's. It was quiet, only a couple of the new witches were here.

And then Charlie.

I went to Art's office and knocked on the door, peeking inside.

Art was sitting at his desk, a cup of coffee in hand and a pet carrier on his desk.

"Come in," he said, his eyes on the pet carrier.

"Uh, Boss?" I asked, stepping in.

"What's up, Billy?" he asked, eyes still on the pet carrier.

I arched a brow, creeping closer. "Uh. What's in the cage?"

"A demon named Biscuit, but Inferna says it's her aunt's naked cat. But this thing is ancient and looks like a crusty mole with eyes that stare into your soul. Somehow we are watching it for the week. I don't know why."

I snorted and went to his desk, leaning down to peek into the cage.

A rattled clicking noise sounded.

"What the fuck?" I mumbled, taking a step back.

"She doesn't like me," Art whispered. "But she loves Calen."

That thing was definitely a demon.

"Well. That's uh... good luck with that," I said. "I came to tell you— there was this guy named Charlie in the elevator, and he said he's invisible, but he's not. And I think he's cracked out on something."

Art shook his head, taking a sip of coffee. "No, Charlie is right. He's a monster, and he is invisible. We can't see him, but I know he comes in and gets work done. Does super solid work, actually. He just likes to keep to himself, so I let him work an earlier schedule. Speaking of, why are you here so early?"

I stared at Art, blinking. "Wait. Charlie is actually invisible?"

Art looked up, arching a brow. "Yes. Just like you're a demon. Just like I'm a witch."

"But I can see him, and so can Jaehan," I said.

"Jaehan? One of our new witches?"

"Yeah," I said.

Art narrowed his eyes on me. "I'm not trying to be an ass, but I don't know what you want me to do with this information, Billy. It's not even 8:30 a.m., I'm babysitting a cat from hell, and Charlie is a solid employee who doesn't seem to have done anything wrong."

True.

Fuck.

"Okay," I said. "Fair enough. Also, is it okay if I work early today?"

"Sure," Art said.

"Actually..." I trailed off, thinking.

Jaehan worked earlier, and so did Charlie. And now I was intrigued by the invisible monster I could suddenly see. "Would it be possible for me to work an earlier schedule going forward?"

Art sighed, his gaze narrowing on me even more. "Yes,

but if anyone asks, I said no, even though you will be leaving early."

I grinned. "Thanks."

He smirked and gave me a little cheer with his mug, but the cat made another clicking noise, and his smile faltered.

"Good luck," I snorted, leaving the office before he could change his mind.

CHAPTER TWO
invisible

CHARLIE

THE DEMON from the elevator stared at me as he came back into the office, making his way straight for my desk in the farthest corner of the room. Of course, no one could see me, so I always sat alone— but now this bastard *could* see me and apparently didn't care about my personal space.

He was a sexy demon who, under different circumstances, I might have enjoyed talking to. I had been watching him around the office for months, damn near leering at him.

There had been moments in the evenings when I saw him walk through shadows. I had caught glimpses of his other form and always wondered about it.

But now I felt very naked in front of him, knowing he could see me. And that wasn't even because I was shirtless.

"Charlie," he said, setting his things down on the desk opposite me.

"What are you doing?" I asked, glaring.

"I have taken it upon myself to pick out a new seat. I'm sorry I said you weren't invisible," he said. "My name is Billy."

"I know your name," I said. "We've been in the same office for months."

"Months?" Billy hissed.

It was absurd to both of us, so I laughed. "Yes, *months*, Billy the shadow demon."

Billy arched a brow, flashing an attractive grin. "So why can I see you now then?"

"I don't know," I lied.

It was a lie because there was only one circumstance in which I could be seen, and I refused to think about it right now.

The possibility that I had stepped into an elevator with the two individuals in the world who were my mates, was *impossible.*

There was the demon, and then there was the witch. The one who was definitely in heat and being irresponsible by waltzing around an office full of hungry creatures.

"You should worry more about your little witch," I said. "The one in heat."

Billy paused for a moment, his six eyes blinking together. "He's not mine."

"Could have fooled me. You growled twice."

"He's not mine yet," Billy corrected. "And I don't mind sharing, you know."

I felt a little shiver of anticipation as he looked me over again.

"You'll have to warm up to me," Billy chuckled. "Is it because I can see you? Or because you apparently don't wear clothing to the office? You know that's some people's nightmare. To come to work without certain clothes on. But here you are, living their nightmare like a happy little dream."

I couldn't help but smile. My tentacles lifted around me, each of them smooth and ending in tapered tips. "Hard to find a shirt when you have this many tentacles."

"That's fair," Billy sighed. "Well, I'm sitting here now. And now we can discuss why we think the little witch and I can see you, a very large tentacled but *invisible* monster."

I stared at him for a moment and then went back to work, doing my best to ignore him. Everything about today was already confusing enough.

"I can't complain about you being half naked," Billy said. "You look...nice."

I smiled a little, trying to focus on the computer screen. I was working on about ten different reports, typing away with three of my tentacles.

It was going to be hard to work with him here. I wanted to do many things to him, to try many things with him.

I scowled. I shouldn't be thinking about that...

"I like how you look too," I admitted.

"Ah. So you *can* give compliments," Billy teased.

"Only sometimes," I said.

Billy stood up again and stretched, his shadowy form drawing my attention again. I stared at him over the top of my computer. There was a window behind his seat, one that reflected us.

It was during moments like this that I could feel I was real when I could see the shape of my reflection. Mirrors didn't show me, but reflections in water and glass did.

I was the figure that humans sometimes swore they saw. A shadow out of the corner of their eyes, a shape in their windows as I walked by. I was a ghost, a monster, a creature that haunted everything that lived.

My existence was a conundrum, but I wasn't the only one like this. There were other monsters like me, ones that existed but didn't exist for everyone.

I liked being that way, observing from the corners as the world spun by.

But now, there was a monster and a witch who could see me. And the witch in heat was going to drive me insane.

Their scent alone made me want to devour them.

I drew in a breath, and even from across the room I could scent the witch. My mouth watered, and my gaze pulled from Billy to him.

He was looking at me. Staring like I was something he knew he shouldn't be able to see but could.

But there was something else there.

Something primal. Something filled with a lust I couldn't simply ignore.

I felt my cock stir and fought off a growl. Fuck.

This was going to be a problem.

How was I going to get any work done like this?

Billy let out a breath. "Fuck. I want him."

"Me too," I admitted before I could stop myself.

Billy turned around in his seat, too, looking at Jaehan. He tilted his head, gesturing for the witch to come to us.

Jaehan shook his head, his expression pinching into a scowl.

"He's very stubborn."

"More like stupid. Every monster in this office is going to be hard for him. He should work from home until his heat passes," I grumbled.

It was simply irresponsible.

"We could help him get through the work day," Billy said.

"As if he would allow that."

"But... if he did. Would you join us?"

I could think of a thousand reasons I should say no to that, and they all would have been a way for me to lie about the truth.

My cock was already getting harder, and all of my frustration from this morning turned into something much darker. My cock could get hard, and no one would see it except the two of them.

"He will say no," I quipped.

At this point, I had stopped typing. I had stopped working. My tentacles moved around me, my cock twitched at the thought of bending the witch over this desk and breeding him.

"Fuck," I muttered.

Billy looked at me, his nostrils flaring. His six eyes glared, and the morning sun coming through the window was blotted out by clouds, casting him in a moment of darkness.

For a second, I saw the form I'd always craved to see. The one that made him look like Baphomet but drenched in darkness.

I wanted to do things to him too. But maybe it was just because this was the first time someone could see me.

Maybe it's because this would be my first time.

The sun came back out, his form turning more human again.

"Charlie," Billy said, his voice a low timbre. "Tell me now. What do you want for breakfast? A demon and a witch? Or some of the fucking bland eggs and toast."

"I've never been with anyone," I said bluntly.

Billy cocked his head. "Really? No one?"

"No one could see me."

"Hmm. Well, even if Jaehan isn't interested, I am. I like the look of your tentacles. And it's not very often that I meet someone much taller than me."

I shivered and looked down. I couldn't control it now. My cock was completely hard and throbbing in my pants.

"Go to the copy room," Billy said, standing up. He leaned over the desk, seeing the hard shape of my cock. "No one ever goes in there, and there is a lock on the door. Go in there and wait."

Fuck. Was I really going to do this?

I was impulsive at times, but that's because I could get away with things. Any time I held something for more than a few seconds, it became invisible too. So I could grab food, drinks, clothes— really anything without anyone knowing.

Did I make a habit of stealing and doing other things?

Maybe, but it was hard to pay for things when no one could see you.

I stood up, my chair moving back. My cock throbbed, my tentacles moving around me as I walked across the office. I walked past Jaehan, ignoring his heated gaze.

The little witch was angry.

His scent made me growl, my cock throbbing harder as I wound through the office until I got to the copy room. It was still early. Not everyone was in the office aside from a few witches and the bosses.

But they would all be busy catching up on emails and drinking coffee, not worrying about us.

I stepped into the copy room, greeted by the scent of warm paper and the soft hum of the fax and printers.

Was I really going to fuck the two of them on the clock?

I sucked in a breath as my cock pulsed again, aching to

be used. I hadn't been this hard in ages, and I was hungry to be touched.

I was hungry to touch.

One of my tentacles slid down, rubbing across my bulge. I shuddered, my entire body reacting.

Fuck it.

Now that the cloud of anger and frustration had passed, I needed to know what was happening.

I needed to know...

Were the demon and witch truly my mates?

CHAPTER THREE

copy room

JAEHAN

I WAS GOING to lose my job, and I'd only had it for a week.

I was in heat and blamed it on the fucking demon who had been stalking me this week and the tentacled bastard in the elevator. Something about being around the two of them had set me off.

Was it the tentacles? Was it the horns? Was it the fact that I was desperate to be fucked by monsters?

I didn't know, but fuck. I could barely think straight.

I just made it out of hell but was throwing myself straight back into trouble.

All of the witches who came in early were like me. They had escaped the evil witches and monsters who had trapped us simply because we were omegas. I had never met this many others in my life, and now that we had escaped— it was nice to know I wasn't alone.

What wasn't nice was the continuous images playing

through my mind of Billy's tongue inside of me while Charlie's tentacles bound me.

My cock hardened, and I released a breath.

"Jaehan," one of the girls whispered. "You should go home."

"I'm fine," I lied.

I wasn't fine. I was sweating and knew at any moment, precum would start to drip from my cock.

"You can't lie to us," she said, shaking her head.

Her name was Ember. She had dark purple hair that fell in long curls with bangs, golden brown skin with a dusting of freckles, and a curvy body that turned heads when she walked in. She was gorgeous and sweet and had fast become a friend.

She was also Cinder's sister. Our HR agent who was dating two employees.

This office was weird, but I couldn't complain. I liked Ember, she was nice. And we had bonded over mutual trauma.

"Seriously," she said, peeking around her computer. "They will understand. Art's mate is an omega. And I'm sure all of them would rather you go home and take care of yourself. Plus, didn't Inferna say we still get paid if we call in for the next few weeks? After everything that has happened, taking a few days to let your body calm down would be good. Also, it's not like my sibling will do anything to punish you. Plus, you're already attracting monsters."

"I don't have anything against monsters," I muttered, ignoring the invisible one as he passed me.

Fuck, his cock was hard.

I turned my head, watching where he went.

No one in this office could see him. That much was, in fact, true.

"Sure, I don't either. My sibling is mated to two of them. But they're going to devour you," she hissed.

I looked back at her and then at the demon that was watching me. Billy.

He nodded his head again, gesturing me to follow him.

Another wave of heat went through me, and I grit my teeth. "Fine," I said, standing up. "Fine. I'm going to do something really quickly and then go home. Can you tell Art for me, Ember?"

She arched a brow and turned her head, looking at Billy and then me again. "Don't fuck him," she sighed.

I damn near hissed at her and grabbed my things, walking in the same direction I'd seen the invisible monster go.

I could feel Billy following me too.

He was my stalker, for fuck's sake, and here I was— letting him follow me.

I rounded the corner, heading down the hall. I could feel the pull now, my veins burning with need. Precum dripped from the tip of my cock, my muscles tensing.

"Don't run," Billy growled behind me. "If you run, I will have to catch you."

Fuck.

A shiver worked down my spine, my heart pounding in my chest.

"Go to the copy room."

There was a part of me that wanted to resist the command, but the rest of me knew I simply couldn't. My feet moved for me, and I got to the end of the hall, going into the copy room.

Charlie turned as I came in, and I was pushed forward as Billy stepped in behind me. My blood rushed in my ears as the door locked behind us.

I was now sandwiched between a six-eyed demon and a tentacled monster, and both of them were hard for me.

Billy stepped close behind me, the heat of his body making me moan. He wasn't touching me, and the tension from not being touched when I wanted to be so badly was enough to make my cock fully hard now.

"I'm in heat," I whimpered. "And it's your fault. Both of you."

"So now what?" Billy asked.

"So now, maybe you'll stop stalking me and just fuck me," I whispered.

Billy was quiet behind me for a moment, but then he stepped closer. I felt the hardness of his cock against my ass, pressing against me.

"Oh, so you've known?" he asked, his words soft and dark.

"Yes," I whispered. I looked up at Charlie, unable to look away. He was beautiful in the most bizarre way and the way he looked at us right now... "Why can we see you? Heats only happen for two reasons. One, it's time for the cycle— and it's not for me. Or two, my mates are nearby."

Charlie stepped closer, one of his tentacles reaching out and tipping my chin up. His body was massive, his muscles stunning. His face was gorgeous, and his eyes reminded me of small galaxies.

"Mates," he said. "That's why you can see me. The two of you are mine."

"Fuck," Billy groaned. "Fuck, I wasn't ready for this."

"Me neither," I breathed, but I still pushed my ass back against him.

He groaned, his clawed hands running up my sides. They dragged over my clothes, my breath hitching.

Charlie's tentacle still held my face tipped up, and he

smiled, revealing a row of sharp white teeth. I felt another tentacle slide up my thigh, the tip tracing over my cock.

"Fuck," I grunted, my head falling back.

"I want to fuck you," Billy growled. "To taste you. You smell like you're ready to be bred."

"Please," I rasped. "It's unbearable."

"I just..." Charlie drifted off for a moment, his eyes darkening. "I just want to be touched. I never have been before."

My heart skipped a beat.

One of my monster mates was a virgin.

My face softened, and I leaned up, surprising us both by kissing him. His lips were soft, and he was a natural, parting them so our tongues could meet.

I groaned and would have fallen forward, but his tentacles wrapped around my waist and steadied me.

I pulled back, the two of us staring. Charlie gave me a little smile, his cheeks turning pink.

"For a big scary monster, you're sweet," I grunted.

I turned around, looking up at Billy. He was in his more human form right now, his skin tan and his black curls that went to his neck. His eyes were completely black, his fangs ready to rip into me.

Part of me wondered what he looked like in the dark. I wanted to be fucked by the scary part of him.

Billy arched a brow, lifting his hand and cupping my jaw. "What are you thinking about, omega?"

"How I want the monster part of you to fuck me," I whispered.

Billy's grip tightened. "Oh? That part of me will give you nightmares."

"Not nightmares," I whispered. More like wet dreams that I would wake up from and immediately cum.

Billy let out a low growl. "Tell us to stop."

"No," I said. "No, I want this. I want to be filled with both your cocks. I want to be held by Charlie's tentacles while you devour me fully. I don't care if we get caught. I'm going home for the day after this."

"Good," Billy said. "We'll fuck you, and then you can go home where you'll be safe."

I whimpered and nodded, thrusting my hips forward and grinding my cock against his. Billy groaned, his head tipping back.

"I promise I will fuck you in my full form after work," he said. "But for now, we will make do. Get his clothes off, Charlie. I will tell you what to do to him."

Charlie's tentacles slid around my waist and undid my belt buckle. Heat flashed through my body again, and I was helpless between the two of them, desperate to be turned into my monsters' fuck toy.

"Please fuck me," I gasped.

My pants fell to the ground, followed by my underwear.

Charlie growled possessively, the sound rumbling through his chest.

"You have to make sure he's slick first," Billy said. He reached up and started to undo his button-down, leaving it open. I reached out and undid his belt and pants, eager to see his monstrous cock.

Fuck. A little moan of desperation left me as one of the tentacles slid down, the tip rubbing over my ass.

Being an omega meant that when I went into heat, my body was ready to be bred and fucked. It meant that his tentacles, his cock, everything, would go in with ease.

I panted and leaned forward, planting my hands on Billy's chest. He stepped even closer, cupping the back of my head and bringing my mouth to his nipple. I immediately started to suck, enjoying the groan that left him. I swirled my tongue and sucked, stifling my noises as Charlie explored my body.

I didn't know either of them. I didn't know anything about them other than they worked for the office and were monsters.

But I knew I had never been this needy in my entire life. I craved to be fucked, to be wanted and touched.

I didn't want to fall in love. I didn't want to be with anyone after everything I had gone through. But this felt right, and I couldn't stop the lust.

I wanted this, even if I didn't want the two creatures who were meant to be my mates.

I sucked harder, only pulling back to let out a cry as Charlie kissed down my spine. His touches were careful, his movements a little unsure. He explored me, his tentacles enveloping me.

Billy tipped my head up, and our lips met in a hungry kiss. He took my hand, sliding it into his pants. I gasped, my eyes widening as I realized there wasn't one cock— but two.

Two cocks.

Charlie spread my ass, running his tongue down it. He swirled it over my entrance, and I damn near came.

"Oh god!" I groaned.

"Did I hurt you?" Charlie asked, pulling back.

"No," I rasped. "No. That felt good. Please don't stop, Charlie."

"Okay," Charlie said, his tentacles now holding me firmly in place.

I wasn't going anywhere now.

Billy growled, thrusting his cocks in my hand. "If Jaehan wants you to stop, he'll ask. And if he can't speak, he'll make this symbol."

Billy showed Charlie and me the symbol, and we both nodded.

"If it's too much, I will say red," I gasped.

"So don't stop until then," Billy chuckled.

I let out a helpless breath, smiling a little as Charlie made a happy noise and started to eat me out again. His tongue pushed inside of me, causing my entire body to arch in pleasure.

Billy sank down in front of me, and I bit my lower lip, fighting a scream as he began to stroke my cock. He leaned forward, scraping his teeth over my hips. The sensation went through me, and I shook my head, tears filling my eyes as the two of them sent me to the edge.

Charlie began to fuck me harder with his monstrous tongue, and then I felt one of his smaller tentacles push inside of me. They worked together in tandem. All the while, Billy took my entire cock into his mouth and began to suck.

"Oh fuck," I gasped. "Oh fuck, oh fuck. I'm going to cum."

I hadn't cum from someone else's touch in so long, and this was primal.

Billy sucked harder, and Charlie's tentacle went deeper, drawing a yelp from me. He didn't stop, didn't slow. Pleasure burst through me, and I shuddered, feeling a hard wave of euphoria crash through me.

Hot ropes of cum shot into Billy's mouth, and he swallowed, still sucking and licking until he'd cleaned up every drop.

I panted, my chest heaving as tears rolled down my cheeks. Charlie pulled his tentacle and tongue free, his hold on me loosening for a moment.

"Bend him over the machine," Billy growled. "Bend him

over the machine and spread his ass so I can show you how to fuck him. Unless he wants us to stop."

"No," I gasped.

Charlie nodded, and I was immediately lifted and shoved across the small room. The copy machine was a massive one. One of Charlie's tentacles lifted the top part, and the machine hummed to life. With the top piece lifted, it was the perfect height to bend me over.

I was slammed on top of it and held in place, one of the tentacles stroking my back like he was petting me. Comforting me before I took Billy's monster cocks.

"I won't give you both yet," Billy grunted. "We'll wait until you take my nightmare form. Are you sure you want this, Jaehan?"

"Yes," I begged. "Please. Please fuck me. Show Charlie how to fuck me."

Charlie stood to my left, his cock straining in his pants. He leaned over, and I could feel him watching as he spread me wide.

"So slick," Billy groaned. "Fuck."

"Please," I whispered.

"Stay still," Billy murmured, dragging his claws down my spine. "Stay still and take it."

CHAPTER FOUR

breeding

BILLY

JAEHAN WAS BOUND by Charlie's tentacles, his ass spread and ready to be taken. I looked up at Charlie, catching his heated gaze.

I needed the workday to be over so the three of us could spend more time getting to know each other's bodies.

"You have a big cock, too," I huffed, letting my pants fall to the floor. "Even though he is practically dripping, he'll need to take every inch carefully."

"Okay," Charlie said, smiling.

Fuck he was pretty.

I smiled at him and then stepped up to Jaehan, gripping my top cock and rubbing the head down his crack. My top cock was nine inches when hard, the bottom one eleven. Even in my more human form, this was a part of me I couldn't hide. My skin was smoky gray, both heads crimson.

He let out a moan, writhing against Charlie's tentacles. "Billy," he groaned.

When I had walked into work this morning, I didn't know I would end up fucking the witch I'd been stalking since I first saw him.

I also didn't know it would be with a virgin tentacled monster who no one else could see but us.

I gripped Jaehan's hips, my claws digging into his skin as I started to ease forward. He sucked in a breath at the first couple of inches, and I slowed, easing forward until half of my cock was inside of him.

"You're so big," he panted. "Ah, fuck. FUCK."

His last cry came from another two inches working into him.

"Two more," I said, gripping him harder.

I wanted to mark him with my claws and teeth. I wanted him to go home today, knowing he had been ravaged by Charlie and me.

I pulled back and then thrust forward. The noise he made caused me to laugh, enjoying how well he took my cock.

"You were made for me," I grunted, thrusting into him. "Fuck. So now you fuck him," I gasped, looking at Charlie.

Charlie watched as I began to pump in and out of the omega witch, my hips moving in a harsh rhythm. I was hungry and needy, and it had been far too long since I had been with someone.

That hunger became a burning flame, one that engulfed me further and further with every thrust.

Charlie moaned and moved closer, a tentacle moving and curling around my neck lightly. I turned and met him with a kiss, sharing the dark needs we both had.

He was a monster like me. A creature, a nightmare. But no one had ever touched him.

No one had ever wanted him.

But I did.

And so did Jaehan.

I fucked Jaehan harder, desperate to fill him with my cum. The need to breed was a primal one, and all I could think about was making him mine.

I groaned, knowing I was about to cum. Jaehan continued to make delicious little slutty noises, his ecstasy apparent. I fed off knowing I brought him pleasure, of knowing I was going to be the one to break his heat this time.

Charlie and I. How would we walk away after this?

I knew I wouldn't.

I'd wanted Jaehan since I saw him, and now that I could see Charlie...

Charlie moved closer, but one of his tentacles bumped against the machine. It hummed to life, causing Charlie to smash the buttons again by accident as he turned.

"Oh no," he gasped.

The flash of light ran under the flat surface, scanning Jaehan's face as I kept fucking him. I didn't stop, couldn't stop, the feeling of fucking him was too good to let go.

"Fuck," Charlie growled, hitting the cancel button a few times.

Jaehan let out a helpless chuckle as the machine started to spit out papers. Each one had a gray scan of Jaehan's face in ecstasy, and now they were scattered around the room like leaves from an autumn tree.

"Fuck, I'm going to cum," I groaned, fucking him harder.

Charlie started to try and pick them up, but I growled.

"Fuck the papers," I snarled. "Watch me fuck him and learn."

I pumped into him over and over until, finally, I came. I cried out, filling him with my hot seed. He groaned as he took it, and I fell forward, leaning over him for a moment to catch my breath.

My other cock was still hard, but I would have to wait. I looked up, glancing at the clock.

It was 8:45 a.m., which meant that pretty soon, the office would not be as empty. And some of the monsters and witches would get here early.

I slowly pulled out, looking at Charlie. "Do you want to fuck him quick, or do you want to wait until later? So you can savor it."

Charlie looked up at the clock, letting out a little noise. "No one can see me if I'm hard, so... I will wait. But I want him first if he is okay with that."

"Yes," Jaehan moaned.

I nodded, wincing. "Sorry, Charlie."

"No, don't be," he said, smirking. "That was educational. Seeing you fuck him... I have ideas. And you make so many noises, omega," he teased, pulling him off the copy machine.

Jaehan's legs started to buckle, but we both caught him, holding him up between us. My cum and his slick dripped down his legs, and he shook his head in a daze.

The three of us looked around the room at the mess we'd made. Papers were scattered everywhere, and I choked on a laugh.

It really had gotten his expression as I fucked him.

"Oh," Jaehan said, letting out a helpless laugh. "Fucking hell, your cock... I want more."

"I have to work," I hissed.

"Can you stand?" Charlie asked.

"I can," Jaehan said.

We both slowly let him go, making sure he didn't fall over.

Charlie shook his head, grinning. "Both of you are ruffled. There's no way someone won't see you and know what's happened."

"They won't know because I'm going home," Jaehan said.

I looked down and realized he was hard again.

"Oh," I whispered.

"I'm in heat," he whimpered, and his scent hit me all over again.

Fuck. I hadn't realized... I could feel his scent affecting my thoughts, making my cock start to harden too.

"We will come over tonight," I said. "After work. Maybe we can leave early."

Jaehan nodded. "I need your numbers, and then I'll send you my address."

"I don't have a phone," Charlie said, grimacing.

We both looked at him like he was an alien.

"Don't you have friends or family to call?" I asked.

Charlie shook his head. "I play games online with some humans, but other than that, it's just me."

My heart squeezed a little, but Charlie shrugged. "I will get a phone."

Jaehan smiled. "Well...good news is that you work with Billy. Maybe you can ride with him...."

"Yes," I said. "Of course. We'll figure it out."

Jaehan let out a satisfied sigh.

The sound of heels clicking echoed, and all three of our heads swiveled over to the door.

Fuck.

"I just need to make a copy really quickly," a voice called.

Not just any voice.

Inferna.

Fuck.

I ran to my clothes, throwing them on as quickly as possible. I would have fallen over as I jumped into my pants, but Charlie's tentacle kept me from doing so.

"Wait," Charlie said. "Fuck. If I touch both of you for a few seconds, you should also turn invisible."

Jaehan and I both stared at him, the clicking getting closer.

"What about all the papers?" Jaehan hissed, leaning over to snatch them off the ground.

I cursed, and we started picking them up, only for Charlie to yank us both to the furthest corner of the room as the door pulled open.

I sucked in a breath, holding it as Inferna stepped in and then stopped.

Her eyebrow arched, her eyes falling to some of the papers.

But she didn't see us.

She leaned down, picking up one of them and holding it up. "For fuck's sake," she muttered, shaking her head in annoyance. "ART!"

The three of us damn near jumped as she turned, leaving the room and walking down the hall.

"Fuck," I hissed.

"Get dressed," Charlie said to both of us.

Jaehan and I finished pulling our clothes on, and then the three of us snuck out of the room, glancing down the hall.

I could practically feel Inferna from here.

"I'm going to the stairs," Jaehan said quickly.

He started to walk away, but I caught up with him, glancing back at Charlie. "I'm going with him," I said. "Stairs are dangerous."

Charlie nodded, knowing what I meant.

Which meant he really had been around working with me for months, and I hadn't realized.

The thought of that made me feel strange and a bit sad.

"I will be fine," Jaehan said, but then he almost tripped on the carpet.

I caught him, hooking my arm in his. "I will go with you to protect you. You forget that not all monsters are nice."

"I didn't forget," he sighed.

But he didn't argue anymore.

The two of us went down the hall quickly, rounding the corner and heading past the elevator. The doors slid open, and I could feel the presence of more witches and monsters.

I could feel eyes on us as I threw open the stairwell door, and we started our descent.

"I'm going to be dead from being so horny by the time you're off work," Jaehan muttered.

"I will bring you food and not one dick, but three."

Jaehan snorted as we hit the next level, continuing down the steps.

"Food, three dicks, and a phone for Charlie."

I smiled to myself. "Fine. We'll stop and get one."

It had been less than an hour, and I was already willing to do whatever the fuck this little omega witch wanted.

CHAPTER FIVE
to be seen

CHARLIE

IN ALL THE months I had worked at this office, even through the chaos of the merger, I had never felt a day drag on like this.

I was eager to be with Billy and Jaehan. The taste I had gotten in the copy room hadn't been enough.

It had almost gotten us in trouble too. Still, ultimately everyone had a team discussion from Art about how we don't play with the equipment. Don't use it for personal use. Don't be a jackass.

Art had a way with dry words at times, but we could all feel the wrath of Inferna bleeding through the ceiling like a punctuation mark to the discussion.

All in all, this was the longest Monday I had ever known in my existence, but it was finally over.

Billy winked at me as we got into the elevator, riding down to the parking garage together. We stood in silence even though I could smell his arousal.

Plus, we both still smelled of Jaehan's heat.

Throughout the day, Jaehan had texted Billy. Eventually, he even sent a couple of photos, ones we had looked at together during a very nice lunch in the bathroom.

"I want my own phone," I said as the doors slid open. "So I can send Jaehan things too. And you."

"We're going to stop to get a phone for you and pick up dinner for the three of us. Do you need to go home for anything? Also, where do you live?" Billy asked.

"Oh..." I trailed off, unsure how to answer that. "Well, I guess you might say I have a roommate. But they don't know I live with them."

"What?" Billy asked, shaking his head. "Seriously? We live in modern times, man."

"Well, no one can see me, so that's hard sometimes."

Billy shook his head again as he led me to his car. "I've never met a creature like you," he grumbled.

I wasn't sure if he meant that as a compliment or not, but I still smiled as I got into the passenger side. It was a tight fit, my tentacles crammed between the door and Billy's shoulder.

"So, is this person a human?" Billy asked as he turned the car on.

"Yes," I said.

The human was named Hunter, and he fully believed he was haunted, but it was fine. He had a great computer set up with games and was about the same size as me, so using his clothes wasn't too bad.

"I'm pretty certain that breaks a lot of laws," Billy mumbled.

"Human laws," I said, shrugging. "I don't know about you, but I don't truly abide by their ways. I don't try to harm anyone, but...some of their ways are annoying. And what laws govern someone who doesn't exist?"

"You do exist," Billy chuckled. "And invisible or not, living with a random human isn't great, I imagine. How do you pay for things? Better yet, how do you get paid?"

"In cash," I answered. "And I will often leave Hunter money, so I don't feel bad about using his things."

There were many mornings I had been drinking carton milk when Hunter had made another surprised yelp after finding a thousand dollars under his pillow. At one point, he had told a friend there was a tooth fairy in the house, but they stole his things and gave him cash. I'd never known fairies to give humans money. They just seemed to trap them and steal their souls, but what did I know?

We had an understanding even though I was no tooth fairy.

Billy snorted. "That's one way to do it."

He started to back the car out but then slammed on his brakes, cursing.

I turned in my seat but saw nothing.

"What the fuck?" Billy whispered. "That was Poppins. I swear I just saw him."

I scowled and looked around the parking garage.

I didn't see anyone, and I certainly didn't see Poppins.

Billy was silent for a moment and then shook his head, muttering to himself.

He continued to back out, and I leaned back, taking a deep breath as we left the garage. Billy stole a glance at me, giving me a soft smile. "You can live with me if you want," he said. "Even if it doesn't work out, you could stay until you figured something else out. But I have a spare room. I have a house in one of the neighborhoods on the east side."

I raised a brow, looking over at him.

I liked him.

I more than liked him.

Even though he had only met me this morning, I had watched him for a while since we worked together. He was quiet sometimes, and for others, he was a force to be reckoned with. All of the things that had happened recently, he had been part of.

He had helped Cinder, who was nice. We had done a one-on-one, and they never acted like I was invisible, even though I was to them.

It was nice to be seen, I realized.

My heart squeezed in my chest. The hole of loneliness I had lived with for so long felt like a stitch had just pulled it closed a little.

How long had I been alive? At least a few hundred years. I had watched humans live their lives and die. I had watched other monsters perish while some continued to gain wealth, and their battles unfold before me.

There were other monsters like me, but we were rare. And wherever I came from, I certainly didn't have a family.

Sometimes I wondered if I was cursed. I wondered if someone had cast a spell over me and if I simply couldn't remember. But there was no way to know.

There were only some things I could remember about long ago, and I didn't keep records.

"Live with me," Billy said again, this time his voice a little more commanding. "Stop living with the human. I don't care what happens, but I don't like the idea of you being alone anymore, Charlie."

I was silent for a few moments, and I looked out the window, watching the city pass us by. I had never imagined that I, a monster, would be working in an office and riding in a car with someone who was fated to be my mate.

I never thought I would have someone I had just met tell me they wanted to see me in a better place.

"Okay," I whispered, swallowing hard. "You don't have to help me, though. I've been just fine on my own."

"You're not on your own anymore," Billy whispered. "I think we've both been around long enough to know how this works. I know that you're mine. I know that I'm yours. And I know that our witch is meant to be with us too. I don't care that I only saw you this morning...." Billy trailed off, turning right into a shopping center. He pulled into a parking spot and turned in his seat, giving me a dark look. "Unless you truly don't want this, don't say no."

I held his gaze, my heart racing. How could I tell him no when this was what I had always wanted?

"Okay," I said. "Thank you. I have money—"

Billy growled, waving his hand. "Shush. I'll be back in about thirty minutes. The phone place is here, and there is a restaurant. We'll be on our way before you know it, and you can finally fuck our little omega."

I nodded, and Billy winked, giving me a rascal smile as he got out of the car. I watched as he went across the parking lot, his human form blending in with the rest of the world.

A tear slid down my cheek, and one of my tentacles lifted, swiping it away.

It hurt to feel like this. It hurt to feel cared for.

What did I offer him? What did I offer Jaehan?

I shook my head, wishing that pain didn't exist. It was sharp, like a knife being dragged across my chest. And the pain was something that was good.

This was good.

I drew in a deep breath and released it, closing my eyes and forcing myself to relax.

Whatever happened, I would forever be tied to these two. And even if they stopped wanting me, I would love them from afar.

I hoped it never came to that, but my decision was made. All of the hesitance I had felt this morning was gone, the frustration turning into a need.

They could see me, and I would do everything I could to prove I could be loved.

CHAPTER SIX

nest

JAEHAN

I HAD MADE a nest in my living room. I had pushed back my couch and coffee table, bringing every blanket and making a place where I could lie and watch tv.

A place where Billy and Charlie could lie next to me.

Nerves worked through me, and I knew I couldn't control what I felt. It was primal, a lust so strong that every breath hurt. My cock had been hard all day, and I had replayed what had happened in the copy room over and over again.

I couldn't stop thinking about Billy's cocks. I couldn't stop thinking about Charlie and his tentacles.

Fuck. I was going to be his first.

The thought excited me while also making me hard again.

A knock echoed through my apartment, and I froze, looking at the door.

It was them.

I knew it was them.

But there was still a moment of fear. I wouldn't be able to fight anyone in my present state. All of the magic that I had would work, but my thoughts weren't clear.

Fuck.

"Jaehan?" Billy called.

I let out a breath and crossed my apartment, unlocking the three spelled deadbolts. I pulled open the door, greeted by the happy faces of my monster co-workers.

My monster mates.

"Hi," I said.

Billy arched a brow, studying me for a moment. "Are you okay?"

"I'm okay," I said quickly. "Come in."

Billy nodded and came inside, hoisting a bag of food up like it was a prize. The smell hit me, making my mouth water.

Charlie hesitated to come inside for a moment, and I looked at him, giving him a soft smile. "Come on," I said, holding my hand out.

He took it, and I tugged him through the doorway, closing the door behind him. I felt my protection spell click back into place, and I reached up— locking everything back.

Charlie made a small noise, his eyes softening with worry. "It concerns me that you live alone."

"I'm okay," I said. "It's gotten better."

Charlie nodded, one of his tentacles winding gently around my waist. I looked up at him, my cock already throbbing.

Fuck, he was beautiful.

"Food first," Billy called from the kitchen.

Charlie smiled, but he still leaned down, offering me a very sweet kiss. I leaned up, meeting him halfway.

His lips fit against mine perfectly, his tentacles giving me a little lift. He grunted, his cock pressing against mine.

I could feel Billy watching us, and that turned me on.

Fuck.

I moaned and pulled back, letting out a helpless laugh. Charlie grinned and wrapped his arms around me, just holding me for a moment.

"You smell like you need to be fucked," he murmured.

"You also smell hungry," Billy growled from the kitchen.

Charlie chuckled and let me go, giving me a little push. "Let's eat. Oh! I have a phone now."

"Good!" I said, going to the kitchen.

Billy had already unpacked the food. He had gotten enough for an entire football team, but I knew both of them could eat.

Before I could grab one of the dumplings, Billy pulled me into a hug, stealing a kiss. I grinned against his mouth, enjoying the way his claws felt over the fabric of my clothes.

"I thought you said food," Charlie teased.

Billy broke the kiss, shrugging. "I had to steal a kiss too. Let's eat. And drink water. Both of you."

I stuck my tongue out at him, which earned me a little warning growl and a pat on the ass.

"This looks good," I said, my mouth watering.

Fuck, had I even eaten today? It was hard to eat sometimes.

"I can hear your stomach growling," Charlie said, shaking his head.

"Did you eat?" Billy asked.

"No, I don't think so," I said, grabbing three plates from the cabinet.

I handed them each one and then started piling food on my plate.

"Did you get the whole menu?" I asked, snorting.

"Yes," Billy said, shrugging. "I've no clue what either one of you likes, so I got it all."

I snorted again, but all of my thoughts were refocused on food. My stomach grumbled, and I sighed, grabbing a set of chopsticks from the bag and leaving the kitchen for the nest.

Charlie and Billy rustled about as they made their plates, the two of them coming to the living room.

Both of them stopped once they saw the nest.

I froze with a mouthful of noodles, looking up at them.

"Did you make this today?" Billy asked.

Heat flushed through me, my cheeks warming. Did he hate it? Did Charlie?

I nodded silently.

"It looks great," Billy said, grinning.

"Can we sit?" Charlie asked.

I swallowed quickly and nodded, blinking back tears. "It's for us."

Billy smiled, and so did Charlie, the two of them stepping inside. They each plopped down next to me, and I let out a sigh of relief.

"It's very comfy," Charlie said.

"It smells like you," Billy murmured.

I smiled, starting to eat again.

The three of us sat in silence, and all of the weird feelings that had bubbled up went away again.

"This is good," I said, gesturing to the food.

"They make great food," Billy said. "They kind of do a

blend of different Asian foods. There is a place I can go next time that is a Korean restaurant, and they have very good bibimbap."

I smiled a little, surprised. "My mother is Korean," I said. "So I grew up eating very good bibimbap and kimchi and hobakjuk. My father is American. And I have a brother too. He's studying abroad right now, though."

"I'd like to meet your family," Billy said.

"I'd like for you to," I said before realizing that might be harder than we realized.

Charlie was silent, and I felt a little tinge of worry. I looked over at him. "We're a family of witches," I said. "They will want to meet you too, Charlie, even if they can't see you. My mother especially will like you, I'm sure. Plus, I think you can be heard, correct?"

"Yeah," Charlie said, his expression easing. "Anyone can hear me."

I nodded.

If or when we got to that, it would be good. My parents were both welcoming to all creatures, our coven too.

"We're part of a coven," I said. "The coven is a good one."

Billy looked up, studying me for a moment. "Can I ask you something?"

"Yes," I said.

"It's about the company."

My stomach twisted a little, but I still nodded. If I was going to date now, then I didn't want to hide anything that had happened.

"How long were you gone?" Billy asked.

Charlie was studying me too now, curious.

I leaned back, balancing my food on my lap. "I was gone a month. I was here when they broke in and took me, which is why the door is impossible to get through now. I don't remember much," I said, swallowing hard.

Just bits and pieces, and all of them were nightmarish.

"My family doesn't know," I said. "When I got out, I told them I had gone on vacation and lost my phone and spent a long time apologizing. I'm the only omega witch part of our coven, and I didn't want them to worry. But... I don't remember much. I remember witches and monsters. And I remember them draining my magic consistently, but I don't know how. I remember seeing some faces here and there. I remember their leader's voice...."

Billy's gaze darkened, his expression becoming unreadable.

"They didn't abuse us necessarily, at least that I am aware of. But they kept us as prisoners. I'm definitely...I have problems now. In fact, I probably shouldn't be dating right now. But I can't stop myself from wanting to be with both of you."

"We can take things slowly," Billy said.

I shook my head. "No. I don't want to go slowly. Even if I weren't in heat, I would want this. There is something special to this, and even though I have my nightmares now, I still want to be with both of you."

"Well," Charlie said, clearing his throat. "The good news is that we monsters are pretty good at fighting nightmares."

I smiled, relaxing. He was like a tentacled knight, wanting to fight off every demon that could hurt me.

One of his tentacles settled on my leg, gentle and caring.

I let out a breath and picked up my plate again, eating.

"I think the three of us all have nightmares," Billy said. "But I'm glad you are safe now, Jaehan. I can't imagine how scary that was. I... I regretted not killing the boss when Cinder and I escaped. We ran into him."

"What does he look like?" I asked, curious.

"A nasty werewolf," Billy sneered, shaking his head. "A predator. Someone who manipulates others and likes to hurt the world. I was more focused on getting Cinder and me out of there, but... knowing what I know now, I would have fought him."

"I think he has something else, though," I whispered. "Werewolves are strong, but if he were just a werewolf, I think he would be dead by now."

Billy nodded, thinking over my words. "Perhaps. Either way, I am concerned. Cinder, Mich, and Lora are safe. Inferna, Calen, and Art seem to be as well. And our group is working together to figure out things and to keep an eye out for anyone that could be a spy."

"Well," Charlie said. "I can help with that. They can't see me. And I have heard many things in passing. Regretfully, I never involved myself, even with some of the things I knew. I feel guilty for that."

"Don't," I said. "You couldn't have known how bad this was. None of you could. We go to work, and we're supposed to be able to clock out and go home, not worry about evil HR agents and corporate spies."

"Maybe I could have prevented some of this," Charlie muttered.

"I could have, too," Billy said. "But... we know now. And we will help. At least, I will. I have it out for a couple of those bastards, Poppins included. I swear I saw him earlier."

A chill passed over me, my stomach twisting. "Poppins," I whispered.

I knew who Poppins was.

"He was... he was there sometimes," I said.

Billy growled, his form shimmering. He had still been in his human form, but now it was slowly melting away.

"I didn't see him earlier," Charlie said, looking at Billy.

"I swear that I did," he said. "I swear."

"I believe you," Charlie said. "But it concerns me that I didn't see him. Or smell him."

Billy nodded, gritting his teeth.

I pressed my lips together and then let out a groan.

I had eaten a lot and now I was full.

"I will take your plate," Charlie said, getting to his feet. "Are you finished, Billy?"

"Yes," he said.

Before either one of us could hand him our plates, two tentacles grabbed them from us. He smirked and left the nest, going to the kitchen.

I let out a breath and then leaned back, spreading out in the sea of blankets. Billy chuckled and leaned back next to me.

"Thank you for dinner," I said.

A wave of sleepiness worked through me, and my eyes fluttered.

Billy made a cute little growl, his hand resting on my side. "Are you sleepy, little omega?"

I didn't want to be. I still wanted to be fucked. But somehow, all of the warm food and then the scents of Billy and Charlie made me want to curl up and sleep.

Charlie came back to the living room and sank to the floor on my other side. He turned over, spooning me. His tentacles wrapped around me, and I found them to be oddly comforting.

I found they made me feel safe.

"Sleep," he said. "I will mate you soon. But I can wait, little one. You are tired, and it has been a long day."

I nodded, but then a flash of fear worked through me.

"Please stay," I whispered.

Billy moved closer to me and pressed my face against his chest. I was between the two of them now, their bodies warm.

"We aren't going anywhere."

CHAPTER SEVEN
terrible tues

BILLY

TUESDAY MORNING CAME TOO FAST, and the three of us woke up in Jaehan's nest not knowing what day it was. I then spent the next twenty minutes getting ready for work, which involved figuring out how to use Jaehan's coffee maker with a weird pod thing.

Jaehan came around the corner, trying to pull on a button-down.

"You can't go to work," I said, looking at Jaehan. "Not like this."

Throughout the night, Jaehan's scent had become even stronger. To the point where I wanted to call in and just spend the day fucking him.

"I have to work," Jaehan said, his eyes pleading.

"No," Charlie said, shaking his head. "I will stay with you today."

I nodded, satisfied with that.

I wanted to stay with Jaehan too, but I also wanted to go into work and see if Poppins was still lurking.

I hadn't slept as I had listened to Jaehan and Charlie in the night. Both of them had slept easily, and I knew that their dreams were good. It gave me a sense of peace.

What didn't give me peace was knowing there were evil bastards roaming around work, and that Jaehan was potentially in danger again.

"I will try to leave early," I said. "But I will be back later tonight either way. Charlie can stay with you and maybe you can finally fuck."

I wanted to be there for that but I could always have them do it again just for me.

Fuck.

Jaehan made a noise but nodded. He looked like he was running a fever, his face and body flushed.

Before the two of them could argue, I pulled Charlie into a kiss, and then Jaehan. I then grabbed my bag and was out the door.

"Help him set up his phone and then text me," I said, shutting it behind me.

It was difficult, but I at least knew Jaehan wasn't alone and that Charlie would be with him.

And I knew I could maybe do some snooping around with Mich or even Anne.

Anne was a great resource for information. She kept a razor eye on everything, was smart, and was good at helping people relax around her.

It took about thirty minutes to get to work through traffic, but I made it just in time.

I stepped off the elevator, my thoughts still turning in my mind.

I wanted to know every fucker in this building who

worked for the enemy. I wanted to track them down and hunt them for hurting Jaehan and other witches.

I could feel eyes on me as I came into the office. I went past the front desk, giving Anne a small wave.

"Hey," she said, smiling at me. "You look like you're on a mission."

"I am," I said, leaning over the top of her desk. "Is Inferna or Art in yet?"

"Not yet," Anne said, glancing at the clock. "It's Tuesday. They usually come in a little later than normal on Tuesdays. Was there something you needed?"

I shook my head, glancing around the office.

Some of the witches were here, already settled in their seats working. I watched them, watching for any sign of something strange.

For any sign of a spy.

"Do we have cameras in the garage?" I asked.

"We do, but only security has access. Well, and I think Inferna might. Or Alex," Anne said. "Why?"

"I think something was taken out of my car," I said, letting the lie roll off the tip of my tongue.

Anne arched a brow, knowing what I said wasn't truthful. "Hmm."

I looked back at her, winking. "Just another Tuesday."

"Indeed," she said, her eyes narrowing further. "Maybe I could show you where the security office is and we can see if they'll let us look?"

"That sounds good," I said.

"Hmm. Let me grab a cup of coffee and then yes. Meet me by the elevators."

"Sounds good."

Within a few minutes, Anne and I were stepping into the elevator and riding down to the first floor.

"I think I saw Poppins," I said, looking at her. "Yesterday. Snooping around."

Her eyes widened, a little hiss leaving her. "Bastard. You'd think he would know better than to be slinking around here. We all know he's involved in this."

I nodded, glaring. "I want to fucking take him out. He was there when they trapped Jaehan."

Anne made a face, arching a brow and smirking.

I pressed my lips together. "Damn it."

She grinned now. "So that's new. Man, all these fucking office romances. Makes me think there's still love out there."

"There is," I said, sighing. "Don't tell anyone."

"Secret is safe with me," Anne said, shrugging. "Let's see if the security bastards will show us anything. Some of them are bad, but I think some of them are good. It's hard to tell."

It was true for Warts & Claws as well. We were surrounded by friends and surrounded by enemies, and it was difficult to tell who was who until the moment something happened.

The elevator slowed and the doors slid open, taking us to the lobby floor. Anne went out and I followed her, the two of us crossing the floor over to a door with the word 'SECURITY' on the front. There was a little centaur with a shield sigil under it.

Anne squared her shoulders, putting on her sweetest composure. It was like watching someone shapeshift right in front of my eyes.

She didn't have the commanding presence that Inferna did, but Anne was just as cunning.

She knocked on the door, the taps echoing through the lobby floor.

I could hear shuffling behind the door, and it opened within a few moments.

A human answered, a bulky man with a mustache. "Yes?" he asked.

Donut crumbs fell from his chin. He wiped them away quickly, arching a furry brow.

"Hi," Anne said. "I wanted to see if you could help us. Yesterday, my employee here thinks he dropped his wallet in the parking garage. I wanted to see if we could take a look at the video to try and see where."

He shook his head, his expression one of disdain. "Nope. Can't show footage to just anyone. You have to have a certain level of clearance."

Anne let out a sigh of disappointment, and I noticed the snakes that made up her hair started to move. They fell out of their bun, but I knew the human couldn't make that out.

I took a small step back.

I had been alive long enough to know not to get in the way of Medusa's granddaughter. Anne was a sweetheart, but she'd also had a few 'accidents' with a couple of monstrous ex-employees.

I wasn't looking to find an early grave.

"I was really hoping a strong man like you would be able to help," she said, her voice soft and hypnotic.

The human gawked at her, his fierce expression melting into one that reminded me of puppy love. Her snakes spread out around her head, a hiss coming from one of them. Each one had scales that varied in color, from brilliant blue to verdant green.

"Yes, yes," he said quickly.

Even if he couldn't see them, the human's survival instincts had kicked in. He didn't know he was face to face with two monsters, but his body did.

"Thanks, sweetheart," she said.

He nodded, letting us both slip inside.

It was a small room that was lined wall to wall with video cameras. My eyes widened as I looked around, realizing they literally had cameras everywhere.

Our floor had its own row of cameras. I took a step closer and winced, realizing the copy room did in fact have a camera.

Fuck my life.

The fact that I still had a job was questionable, but overall our company seemed to turn a blind eye to sex in the office. For obvious reasons.

But still.

"Where do you think you dropped it?" the human asked.

He squeezed past Anne and me, going to the section of parking garage cameras. I moved up behind him on his right, Anne on his left. I leaned in a little closer, inspecting all of the screens.

They could see everything. Everything that happened in this building.

I had known there were cameras everywhere but it hadn't truly registered that they were watching everything. The only room on our floor without a camera was the bathroom and the shifting room.

Fuck.

"I think it was over on this one," I said, pointing to the area I parked in yesterday.

"What time?"

"Around 6 p.m."

"Hmm," he sighed.

He leaned forward and started tapping buttons,

entering in dates and times. Within a few moments, we were watching footage of yesterday.

"I'll start at 5:30 p.m.," he said. "Sometimes people misremember times so if something like this happens, we search within a time range. Also, please don't tell anyone I helped you. I could get in trouble."

"I won't," I lied.

Anne gave the human a little pat of comfort. "Don't worry, sweetheart. We just need to find his wallet."

He nodded, leaning in and tapping a few more buttons.

The camera was moving at a quicker speed now, but we were still able to see everything that happened. I fought off a chuckle as we watched people walk by. They looked like waddling ducks when they were moving on camera.

I narrowed by eyes and then sucked in a breath.

Poppins.

Fuck.

The bastard walked right by my car, but then stopped.

"Can you let it go at normal speed?" I asked, trying to suppress the tension in my tone.

He clicked a button and it slowed.

The bastard was at my car and within a few movements, popped the trunk. My stomach twisted as I watched him rummage through it.

What the fuck was he looking for? What was he doing?

Anne stole a nervous glance at me, her eyes wide.

Poppins pulled something from his pocket, dropped it in my trunk, and then slammed it shut. He then looked over his shoulder and moved away, just as I walked up.

It looked like I was alone, but I knew that Charlie was with me. The door opened by itself and the security guard leaned in, scowling.

"How the hell did your door open like that?" he asked.

"Oh, there's a remote," I said, making a face.

"Oh," he said, frowning. "Okay. Well it doesn't look like your wallet was dropped. Who was that guy in your trunk?"

"Oh, just a friend," I said, looking at Anne.

She gave a little nod, smiling at the human. "I guess he didn't drop it yesterday. Thank you for taking a look."

He nodded, his cheeks turning bright pink as he looked at her. "You're welcome."

Anne and I both turned, leaving the room quickly. We were both silent as we went back to the elevator, the tension of knowing that bastard had planted something in my car growing.

The elevator doors slid open and we both stepped inside. Once they closed, I let out a growl.

"God damn it," I snapped.

Anne hit the parking garage floor button, shaking her head. "Let's go see if we can find what was in your car."

"I just don't understand," I growled. "It doesn't make any sense as to why he would have been there. This is too fucking much."

"It is," Anne said. "But I would rather be involved and know what is going on. I'd rather be on the side we are on than not."

"I'd rather not be a target though," I grumbled.

The doors opened again and we went out into the garage, greeted by the smell of cars. I wasn't a fan of the parking garage for that reason alone, the scent always lingering.

Everyone was up in the office by now and it was quiet. I took the lead, taking us to my car.

We both stared at the trunk for a moment and I reached in my pocket, pulling out the keys.

"What if it's an explosive?" Anne asked.

"Come on," I sighed. "There's no way. I mean, we're at an office for crying out loud."

"Yes, but it's not a normal office. It's one with monsters and witches and corporate villains, and not the sexy ones."

I rolled my eyes, but I was nervous too.

I took a deep breath and exhaled, stepping up to the trunk. I clicked the unlock button and it popped. I stared for a moment, waiting to see if the two of us were blown back to hell, but nothing happened.

I scowled and slowly lifted the trunk, peeking inside.

There was only one thing inside. A note.

I felt a chill work down my spine, my heart pounding. I snatched it up and slammed the trunk, unfolding it. Anne crept closer, looking over my shoulder.

They are coming for all of you and they will kill every last omega in the office if they can't have them. Warn Inferna.

I held the note, staring at it and rereading it. Looking over each word, looking for something that didn't feel so damn ominous.

Anne let out a shaky sigh. "Well, let's go find Inferna. She'll want to see this."

CHAPTER EIGHT

tentacle tuesday

CHARLIE

JAEHAN and I had breakfast together and set up my phone, taking a selfie together and sending it to Billy. The morning had been nice, but I was finding it harder and harder not to be...hard.

Jaehan's scent was addicting and I wanted to taste him. I wanted to explore his body with each of my tentacles, to wrap him up in them while I used him. While I worshiped him.

He let out a groan from across the room, his head tipping back. He had just gotten out of the shower and was dripping, a towel wrapped snugly around his waist.

I watched him, my cock pulsing.

I had never been with someone. Knowing he would be my first made my stomach flutter. It also made it even harder to control myself.

I was patient though. Even with his scent tempting me. Even with his body dripping, begging to be licked. He was in heat, he was in need, but I wouldn't do anything until he asked me to.

I wanted to make sure he wanted this. After everything he had been through, I wanted to make sure he knew he had control.

Jaehan looked at me from across the room. His black hair was damp, a couple of drops falling and rolling down his muscles. He was lean, his beige skin glimmering as if he'd been dusted with light.

"Magic?" I asked, cocking my head.

Jaehan nodded, his eyes heating. "My magic is very close with elements. So sometimes, when I take showers, I will glow a little after. It washes my body, but it also brings my magic closer to the surface."

I was intrigued by that.

Jaehan walked over to me, his towel still clinging to his hips. He stepped into the nest, now almost standing over me.

I looked up at him, my head tipping back. One of my tentacles reached up, curling around his ankle.

I could feel the hum of his magic now. It was strong, intense.

"Are you going to touch me?" he whispered.

"Yes," I said, swallowing hard. "If you want me to, Jaehan."

"I want you to," he said.

He stepped closer now, straddling me. I stared up at him, enchanted. He was a spell I never wanted to escape, a wish I'd always dreamed of catching.

"Jaehan," I whispered, swallowing hard. "I want you."

"Then take me," he murmured.

He let go of his towel and it fell to the side. His cock was free now, hovering right in front of my face.

I immediately gripped it with one of my tentacles, winding it all the way around his shaft. There were small ridges along the underside, suckers that would grip his skin.

Some of my tentacles were smooth, some had ridges, and others had suckers. I was a monster, a creature with no true definition.

But I knew one thing now.

I was Jaehan's. I was meant to be his.

A low growl left me and I pulled him forward, taking the head of his cock between my lips. He cried out, his hips jerking forward.

He tasted good, a drop of precum on my tongue. I groaned as I started to suck, stroking him with the tentacle as I used my mouth.

It felt right to hold him like this. More of my tentacles wound up his body as he gasped, tugging apart his legs so I could explore every part of him.

My cock pulsed now, desperate to fill him. But I would need to warm him up first.

I would need to make sure he was ready for me. My cock was large and compared to my body, he was small.

The tentacle on his cock slid away and I took his shaft down my throat. He cried out, his fingers knotting in my hair. He held my face to him, my air dying. But fuck, the flood of euphoria running through me now was worth it.

He thrust harder, his little hips going wild even as I controlled his body. He was like a puppet, but he was still the one fucking my throat.

He pulled back and I dragged in air, letting out a hungry noise.

"If you need to stop, say red," I rasped. "Like Billy told us."

"Yes," Jaehan cried. "Fuck. Your tentacle on my ass feels amazing."

"I have to warm you up," I grunted.

He nodded, his expression warping with pleasure as I pulled him down into the nest. I rolled him over onto all fours, shoving his face down into the blankets.

Fuck. Everything about him was perfect. His ass faced me, his legs parted by my tentacles. His cock was hard and throbbing, his balls smooth and begging to be touched.

His ass was mine.

The scent of his heat rushed over me again, the monstrous part of me rising up. I wanted to devour this little omega, to breed him until his heat finally broke. I would fuck him over and over again today until Billy got home, and then Billy would fuck both of us into the night.

"I want to take pictures," I said, staring at his body. "I want to always have this."

Jaehan nodded, groaning. "Take them and send them to Billy."

I grabbed my phone and continued to play with him with my tentacles. Every noise he made was perfect, his body writhing in my grasp.

I opened the camera and smiled, taking a picture of him spread wide and bent over. My cock throbbed as I snapped a few more, sending them to Billy.

BILLY: FUCK

Jaehan said we should show you

Billy: Fuck I wish I were there. Take video of you fucking him, have one of your tentacles hold it

Okay.

Billy: Have fun, I can't wait to see you fuck him again later

I smiled and took my phone with one of my tentacles, turning it to video. It snaked around, setting the phone to the side so that the video would show all of Jaehan and my cock and tentacles.

Jaehan groaned as I started to milk his cock with one of my tentacles. I moved closer to him, unbuttoning the top of my pants and pushing them down. My cock sprang free, slapping against Jaehan's skin.

He turned, sucking in a breath as he saw it.

"Fuck, Charlie," he whispered, his eyes wide.

My cock was eleven inches with ridges along the bottom and suckers along the top. The head was tapered and already dripping with precum, desperate to fill Jaehan.

Fuck. I let out a low groan, reaching down to stroke it. I ran my palm over the tip, using the precum to lube up the head.

"I'm already slick," Jaehan gasped. "Just go slowly. Fuck, it's so big and it's not even inside of me yet."

"You'll take it," I said, knowing that he would. "The suckers will lubricate too, and the lubrication will make you high. If you ever taste it, it'll make you feel good. And with your omega heat...I don't know what will happen."

"Fuck me," Jaehan rasped, looking over his shoulder. "Fuck me like the monster you are. I want you to breed me, to fill me. I want you so fucking badly. My cock and ass are yours, Charlie. Please. If I need you to stop then I will say so."

"Okay," I whispered, my muscles tensing.

I rubbed the head of my cock down his ass, pressing

against his entrance. He let out a long moan as I began to push inside of him, the feeling of finally fucking something other than my hand or tentacles making me shiver.

"Oh," I gasped, my head tipping back.

Pleasure unlike anything I'd felt before worked through me, a wave that I couldn't control. I eased into him more, his body pulsing tightly around me. He let out a cry, his breath hitching as he pushed his ass back more.

"Fuck," we both said together.

He took inch after inch, every ridge and sucker. My hips flexed, my control starting to slip more and more. All of my tentacles wrapped around his body, binding his arms to his sides and teasing his cock.

I held his torso up now, reaching around and stroking his shaft as he took another inch.

He cried out, his head falling forward. I used another tentacle to grip his head, yanking it back.

"I want a tentacle in my mouth," he gasped. "Please. I don't want you to stop. Fuck, you feel so good."

His request was one I couldn't deny. Another tentacle snaked around to his mouth. He parted his lips with a grunt and I didn't hesitate to fill him.

"Mine," I growled. "You're fucking mine."

Jaehan nodded, his throat contracting with muffled groans as I started to fuck him in a rhythm. My hips slammed forward, giving him the last inches of my massive cock. He screamed, but my tentacle inside his mouth thrust down his throat.

I began to move, my hips finding a hungry rhythm. Primal urges overcame me, my thoughts melting into nothing but pure carnal lust. He was my omega, my mate, my toy to fuck and use.

I groaned as I took him, slamming in and out of him. His

body was limp in my tentacles, taking everything I gave him like a good omega.

I pulled the tentacle free from his throat and he gasped, dragging in air.

He grunted, his words coming in pants. "Choke me," he rasped. "Choke me while you fuck me."

The tentacle that had just fucked his throat wrapped around his neck, careful to only squeeze the sides and not his Adam's apple.

My cock slammed into him harder and I closed my eyes, losing myself to him. I could feel his magic, his slick, his fucking soul begging me to breed him.

I growled, rutting him into the blankets of our nest. I lowered him down beneath me, fucking him harder and harder as I choked him.

I let up, allowing him to breathe.

Fuck. What were all of these thoughts and urges? I wanted to do so many things to him, his heat driving me crazy. It was brutal, this type of pleasure a torrent unlike anything I'd ever experienced before.

He cried out over and over until finally, I knew he was close to cumming. I pulled out of him and flipped him over onto his back, immediately slamming back inside of him.

Jaehan screamed, his eyes rolling back in ecstasy. I leaned down, meeting him in a hungry kiss as I gripped his cock between us and stroked. Our tongues fought, the taste of him something that would live in my memories forever.

Tears slid down my cheeks and I knelt my forehead to his. Every breath was shared, our bodies bound together.

"Charlie," he rasped. "Oh fuck. Fuck, you're going to make me cum."

"Cum for me," I growled. "Please."

He nodded, his pants becoming more rapid as I stroked

him faster and faster. He writhed beneath me, his spine arching as he let out a loud scream.

I looked down right as his cock started to cum, his hot seed shooting out onto the two of us. I stroked him faster until every drop spilled free, and then I wiped it up with a tentacle and brought it to my mouth.

Fuck. He tasted like heaven.

I groaned, slowing my rhythm into rough thrusts. Each one, he took all eleven inches before I dragged my cock back out and took him again.

I tilted my head back, moaning.

"I want you to fill me," Jaehan whimpered. "Please. Please fill me."

Another request I couldn't say no to.

CHAPTER NINE

curses

JAEHAN

I WATCHED in wonder as my tentacled mate thrust into me one last time, letting out a long growl as he started to cum. I gasped as I felt his seed fill me, all of the heat flooding me.

My head was swimming and he was right. His cum made me feel like I was floating in the clouds.

He finally stopped moving, his lungs heaving in pants. His pale skin had flushed in some places, his long hair draping around his face.

His tentacles became gentle now, loving. His eyes widened as he looked down at me, as if realizing what we had just done.

I'd never been fucked that hard in my life. Tentacles were possibly my new favorite thing.

I leaned up, wrapping my arms around his neck and pulling him into a gentle kiss. He melted against me, his breaths softening.

I let him go, collapsing into the blankets.

"That was...." I drifted off, wiping sweat from my forehead. "Fuck. That was beautiful."

Charlie nodded, his expression softening as he collapsed next to me. One of his tentacles reached over, grabbing the phone that had just recorded our fist time together.

The thought of that turned me on.

He handed me the phone, making a little noise. I fought off a laugh, looking over at him.

"Are you okay?" I snorted.

He nodded, grinning. "I can't even speak. You're beautiful, Jaehan."

His words melted me and I smiled, stopping the video. It was a long one too, and the angle showed just enough of everything to be perfect.

"Can I send it to Billy? And to myself?" I asked.

"Please," Charlie huffed, making a satisfied hum.

I sent it to my phone and to Billy, smirking as I watched it go to our demon mate.

I wanted him too. I wanted to fuck him as soon as he was home, to feel what his two cocks would be like.

Heat flared through me again even though I had just been wrecked, making both Charlie and me groan.

"Not satisfied," he chuckled.

"Satisfied," I said, rolling over onto his chest.

I cuddled him closer, pressing my face against his chest. We smelled like sex, my body soap and our nest.

I listened to his heart pound, closing my eyes as the rhythm relaxed me.

"You took every inch," he said. "I was proud."

I grinned like an idiot. "You have a very...interesting cock."

Every ridge and sucker had been both torture and heaven.

One of his tentacles slid down my side, curling around my hip.

Heat burned through me again, my cock starting to harden.

Fuck. I had just cum so much, but I wanted him again.

Charlie lifted his head, looking down at me. He made a *tsking* noise, settling back down.

"You like to be praised for being good."

I nodded, swallowing hard. It was true. I liked being told I was good, to hear that everything that happened had been amazing.

"You did so well taking my tentacle down your throat too," he said. "Thrusting in and out of you. You just let me use you over and over again like a good little slut."

My cock hardened even more and I bit my lower lip.

A tentacle with suckers slid over my chest, the tip curling over one of my nipples. The moan that left me was involuntary, my eyes fluttering with another wave of ecstasy.

He flicked it, teasing it. One of the suckers gripped my skin, tugging on it.

"Charlie," I rasped. "Fuck."

Charlie growled, his tentacles wrapping around my entire body and lifting me. He pulled me into a straddle over his hips, my cock pressed against his abs.

I stared down at him, the fever returning with a vengeance.

"I'm going to fuck you again," Charlie said, smiling. "Once simply isn't enough. You feel so fucking good, Jaehan."

I nodded, my breath hitching. I loved how his tentacles felt as they wrapped around me, the suckers pulling on my nipples. My head fell back as he toyed with me, warming me up.

I was going to cum again just from him playing with my nipples.

"Use me," I rasped. "Use me again. Please."

"No," Charlie said. "Not yet. I'm just enjoying hearing you moan. Watching your cock throb with need. You're such a hungry little omega."

"Please," I groaned, my hips grinding.

His tentacles tightened around me, holding me in place. A low growl came from him, his fangs glistening as he smirked.

"I have so many things I want to do with you," he said. "So many things I want to try."

"Like what?" I rasped, my cock now as hard as it could possibly be.

He continued to torture my nipples, rubbing them in small teasing circles.

"Hmm... Do you really want to know?"

"Yes," I moaned. "Fuck. I want to know everything. I want to know everything you want to do. Your kinks, your likes, your desires. Everything."

I felt Charlie's cock start to harden, his shaft long enough to rub against my ass and lower back. My stomach fluttered, the thought of taking him again exciting me.

I had things I wanted to do. Dark desires that I never shared with anyone, because I'd never met anyone I could trust.

But it was different with him. It was different with Billy. There was a connection between the three of us that I couldn't ignore, and didn't want to ignore.

I had found my mates. I was in heat. They wanted me, would protect me.

"I can tell you what I want," I said, looking down at Charlie.

Fuck, he was beautiful. The way his skin glittered in the sunlight like freshly polished opal, his eyes reminding of a rainbow. His hair was splayed out, his muscles smooth, his jaw and cheekbones chiseled.

He was gorgeous.

"What do you want?" Charlie asked, his smile softening.

"I want you to use me however you want," I said, my voice lowering. I swallowed hard, feeling like I was about to reveal secrets about myself. "Even if I'm asleep, I want you to touch me if you want to. We would talk about consent and everything beforehand but....I like the idea of waking up from a dream wrapped in your tentacles."

Fuck, even saying it aloud was enough to make me shiver.

"I want you to chase me. To trap me. I like to be praised, but I also like... a little bit of fear. I want to be a little scared, and I know that I trust you so I would be safe and wouldn't be harmed. I want you to fuck me even if I beg you to stop," I whispered, precum dripping from my cock. "Those are the things I want."

Charlie made a hungry noise, pulling me down for a heady kiss. I moaned, parting my lips for him before he broke it, lying back again.

"Those all sound like things I would like to do," Charlie said, a soft growl following his words. "I like the idea of those things, but I would like to wait for Billy."

I nodded. "I agree. Well...I want him to do those things too. Maybe both of you."

Charlie chuckled. "Indeed, it would be fun."

"What do you want?" I asked.

"All of what you said and a little more. I like the idea of breeding you until you can't think straight. And I like the idea of sounding your cock with one of my smaller tentacles."

My eyes widened, the thought never crossing my mind. Perhaps there would have been a time when I would have been horrified at the idea of something going into my cock, but the idea of his tentacle being what did it, turned me on.

"Really, I'm a monster, my love. I have tentacles, I have a breeding kink, my cum will make you high, and the scent of fear turns me on. I think we might do well together."

"I think so," I whispered, swallowing hard.

"And so, for now I'm going to fuck you again. And I'm going to make you eat food after that, and then fuck you again and again until our mate gets home. And then I'm going to see what happens when you have two monsters that trap you and breed you. Sound good?"

"Yes," I grunted. "Sounds more than good."

BY THE TIME Billy came home to us, I had been fucked four times. If Charlie didn't fuck me with his cock, it was with one of his many tentacles. After the fourth time, we had showered together and had gotten ready for the return of our demon.

Billy stepped inside, letting out a loud groan. "Fuck. This whole apartment smells like sex."

Charlie and I were cuddled on the couch, but I sat up with a stupid grin.

I was unreasonably happy that he was home. I took a

deep breath, feeling even more whole now that he was here too.

Home.

Fuck, I was really invested at this point.

Billy walked over to us, setting down his bag. I stood up, meeting him in a big hug.

He held me tightly, and even though we weren't fully bonded yet, I could feel his worry.

"What's wrong?" Charlie asked.

Billy's arms tightened around me a little more. "Today, we learned more things that are concerning. I need to fill you both in on them, but I'm worried. And hungry."

"I ordered food," Charlie said. "Should be here soon. Jaehan showed me how to use an app that delivers it."

I snorted, looking back at him. "For someone who works on apps, your lack of understanding of everything is confusing."

He grinned, shrugging. "I am a bit stuck in the past sometimes, I suppose. But task reports are easy and it's more about testing bugs, not using the app."

"It's endearing," Billy said, kissing the top of my head.

I buried my face in his chest, breathing in his scent. "You should shift," I whispered, feeling the tension still. "You feel tense."

"I am," Billy said. "And yes. I think my human form is tired. And it's exhausting to hold it for so long some days."

I took a step back from him, and then laughed as two tentacles tugged me back onto the couch next to Charlie.

Billy smirked and then shifted, allowing his form to change.

Charlie and I both watched, a little too excited to see him in his monster form.

His upper half became drenched in shadows, his lower

half reminding me of a satyr. He must have had enough magic to allow his clothes to change sizes with him, because they adjusted to his new, even larger body.

The lights in the apartment flickered, the moments of darkness showing us an even more beastly form.

"Hi," I said, grinning.

Charlie let out a happy sigh. "You are magnificent in the dark."

"Scary," Billy teased.

He joined the two of us on the couch, relaxing into the cushion.

"Today was a mess. You know how I thought I saw Poppins yesterday?"

"Yes," we both said.

"Well, he was there. This morning, Anne and I managed to get a look at security footage of the parking garage. We saw on camera that Poppins put something in my car, so we both went down to investigate."

My stomach twisted, my heart beating faster.

"We opened my trunk, and I found a note he had left. It said 'They are coming for all of you and they will kill every last omega in the office if they can't have them. Warn Inferna.' Which is rather ominous. So of course, Anne and I went to Inferna with the note. She was furious. Not only because of Poppins, but everything. We called a small meeting in the shifting room and talked through plans and things we can do. I did tell them that the three of us are seeing each other, and that I am concerned for your safety. Inferna said you both could take off the rest of the week and stay out of the office with pay. The last couple of times, bad things have happened, so I'd like to do as much as possible to avoid that. Whatever we can all do to stay safe is the best. I hope you're both okay that I told them we're seeing each other."

"I am," I said.

"Do they even know who I am?" Charlie snorted.

"Some of them did, which then we all had a random conversation about you. Lora was bothered that she's never seen you since she is fae, and they notoriously can see everything."

Charlie shrugged. "Sometimes I think I'm cursed."

We both looked at him, the thought making me scowl.

Billy hummed to himself. "Have you always been invisible?"

Charlie shrugged again. "I dont know. It's hard to say. I don't remember a lot of things prior to this century."

I didn't like the sound of that.

"At some point, we should see if you are spelled," I said. "My mother is very good with such curses and could help."

Charlie smiled, giving me a soft look. "I'd like to meet your mom, but I don't know how I would feel about being visible. But maybe."

"It could be causing other things though," Billy said. "Like memory loss."

He sighed with a grunt. "Fine. We will worry about that later."

"This weekend, I'm supposed to go see them," I said, the thought crashing in.

Fuck, I'd forgotten about that with everything that had happened between now and yesterday morning.

"Well, if we survive, then we can all go. If you want, of course," Billy said.

"We will be okay," Charlie growled. "It will be fine. I'd like to see them try to harm either one of you."

"It's not me or you that I am concerned about. It is our omega," Billy said, looking down at me.

Even though his face was in shadows now, I could still see his six eyes watching me. Concerned. Worried.

"I will be okay," I said, leaning back into the couch cushion. "I am not helpless. I know it may seem that way since all I can think about is sex right now, but my magic is quite strong. They just caught me off guard last time. It won't be that way again."

That much, I was determined.

"I am concerned for the others though," I said, thinking about the other witches in the office.

Like Ember. Ember had wonderful magic, but it was not combative. It was healing, the kind that made crops flourish and the sky a little more blue.

It wasn't fighting magic though, and I wasn't sure who would protect her.

Who would protect any of them? I had two monsters now...but not everyone did. Not everyone was fated to two fierce creatures.

"So," Billy said. "I will go to work again tomorrow, but... I'm snooping around some. Investigating, keeping an eye out for anything suspicious."

"I don't like that," I said. "They could do something to you. You're strong but you're not invincible."

"I am a very powerful demon," Billy said. "Very powerful. I have no need to do the things I do, such as working for this company, but I do because I want to. But before this was ever an option, I spent most of my time in the courts of hell or here on earth. I've gone through a lot of changes, as many monster have in the last fifty years, but they would be stupid to try and do something to me."

"But they've caught you before," I said. "With Cinder. That's what I heard."

Billy was quiet for a moment and then nodded. "They did."

I was tense now. Billy was strong, but so was I. And they had caught me and kept me in a magic coma of some sort until I was released. They had caught him before, and while he had escaped, the creatures involved in this would get better. Wiser.

"Okay," Billy sighed. "I will be careful. And I won't be alone, my little omega. I promise."

I let out a sigh, still worried.

Charlie chuckled. "He's very convincing when he has that expression."

"Indeed," Billy muttered, shaking his head. "So. That was my day. Now tell me every little detail about what I missed today."

CHAPTER TEN

teamwork

BILLY

THERE WEREN'T VERY many things that surprised me anymore, but hearing that both Charlie and Jaehan's kinks lined up with my own did. The thought of them fucking all day today made me hungry to breed Jaehan too, and to finally fuck Charlie.

He was still a virgin in other ways and it was only fair that I got to be the one to take it.

Charlie winked at me, his grin devious.

Jaehan was still sitting between us on the couch, talking about his likes and dislikes. We had established our boundaries, had talked through safe words again, and now...

Now I wanted to play.

Jaehan wanted to be fucked and bred and used.

I could help with that.

Both of my cocks began to harden, the thought of chasing him like prey making me lean forward.

"I have an idea," I said. "One you can say no to, of course."

Jaehan cocked his head, his eyes a little wide with nerves and excitement.

"I have a house in one of the neighborhoods, and not too much farther is a massive park. How do you feel about a little chase? We can sleep at my house tonight and both of you can stay there tomorrow."

Jaehan hesitated for a moment, his eyes moving to the nest he'd made.

I felt a little trace of worry. "We can bring the nest, my love. You did very well on it. This way we will have more space though, and Charlie could even set up his room maybe. You can say no."

Jaehan looked at Charlie and then to me. "I want to. But the nest has to come."

"Yes," Charlie agreed. "We will bring the nest. And I think a chase sounds wonderful. It has been a long time since I have been in the woods, and I like the idea of catching you."

I met Charlie's gaze again, an unspoken agreement forming.

We would trap him together. Herd him like a lost little pet.

Fuck.

"Get dressed," I said, giving Jaehan a gentle pat. "Pack your things. Charlie and I will get the nest into my car. Does that sound good?"

"Yes," he said, beaming.

"Good," I said, watching as he got up and went to his room.

I looked at Charlie, the two of us sharing a wicked smile.

"How are you feeling?" I asked him.

Charlie slid closer, one of his tentacles running over my thigh. "Good. Very good. I want... at some point, I want to do things with you too."

I nodded, the thought making my cocks pulse. "I'm going to fuck you," I said. "Don't worry. And Jaehan can watch."

Charlie smirked and leaned closer, the two of us kissing. I groaned, melting into it.

I had always believed I would never find love. As a demon, there were many of us who were raised to believe love was not for us. Humans, witches, other monsters and creatures— their love was not meant to be for me.

But that was a lie.

Love was meant for everyone. Having a relationship wasn't meant to be gatekept, even if you were an ancient demon.

"Let's get the nest," I whispered, breathing in Charlie's scent. "Before I say fuck my grand plans and take you now."

Charlie's tentacle pulled back and he let out a soft laugh, standing. "Tempting. But I like the idea of the forest, so I will be patient."

THE MOON HALOED the trees that loomed around me, but it didn't quite reach the forest floor. Shadows moved with me, the darkness clinging to my monstrous form.

The three of us had made it to the park within a couple of hours. Now, it was late enough that all of the humans had gone— leaving us with land that, for the most part, would be empty of others.

I could feel the animals moving around me, giving me a wide berth.

It was in the darkness that I was strongest, and they knew that a monster had come to their home tonight.

Charlie and I had made a plan. We had sent Jaehan in, and would circle him from opposite sides. If Jaehan needed to stop or needed help, he would text one of us and we would go to him immediately.

But, other than that, we would hunt him.

He was just a little witch, one in heat and begging to be fucked by two monsters who wanted to devour him.

A low growl left me, my form now fully shifted. Horns stretched above my head, my six eyes blinking. I could see perfectly, could hear and smell everything around me.

I could smell his heat.

My cocks hardened, extending from their sheaths.

"Little witch," I whispered, my voice a drawn-out growl. "*Run.*"

I could hear his heart hammering in his chest. If he wasn't there now, soon he would fall into a place of knowing he was the prey. His instincts would kick in, his body knowing that what hunted him meant to eat him.

Even if it was what he wanted, his body would still resist. His survival instincts would force him to run.

Just what I wanted. What I craved.

After everything that had happened today, unleashing the beast inside of me was thrilling.

I heard the cracking of twigs, Jaehan's breath becoming quicker. He was moving faster through the woods now, going in deeper.

I followed him, giving him enough space to not be able to see me, but still letting him know I was here.

I was hunting him.

Charlie was ahead of him, which he didn't realize. He would wait until I gave the signal, and then we would play.

"Little witch," I growled. "An omega snack. Just for us."

His breath became a pant and he moved a little faster. I chuckled and started to run right behind him, allowing my shadows to tease forward.

I could see him now, dashing through the trees like a desperate deer. He looked back over his shoulder, his eyes widening.

My little witch couldn't hide in the darkness. His magic was too bright, his soul like a lit flame.

I growled, moving faster. Getting closer.

He let out a panicked yelp, and I caught the scent.

The scent of fear.

Fuck.

Both of my cocks were fully hard now and it was painful to run. To chase. I could feel the blood pumping through my body, the need to fuck him growing stronger.

"*Now*," I snarled, knowing that my voice echoed through the forest.

Tentacles burst from the trees, grabbing Jaehan and lifting him. He fought, a bug trapped in a web. He screamed, his voice echoing as my shadows consumed everything.

The moon couldn't reach us now. The darkness spread around us, a blanket over all that lived.

"Little witch," I snarled, the sound of my hooved feet crunching over twigs and leaves. "I'm going to fuck you."

"No," he rasped. "No, no. Let me go!"

His begging was like music, the scent of his fear making me groan. The tentacles that bound him weren't budging, holding him in place even though he squirmed.

Charlie emerged from the darkness, a low growl leaving

him. He truly was a monster, a beautiful one. One that even made me feel a prick of worry.

I realized that he had other forms too, and this one...

This one was terrifying.

Jaehan let out a scream, his head turning as he looked at me and then around.

He hadn't seen Charlie yet.

Charlie slowly turned him, and Jaehan froze. His scent heightened, the sound of his heart thrashing in his chest becoming an anthem to our dark game.

"What are you?" He rasped.

Fuck. His fear was delicious. I crept closer, my eyes moving back to Charlie.

Charlie was twice as large as before, with twice as many tentacles. His rainbow eyes had multiplied, and his mouth had unhinged, showing a jaw full of sharp teeth. His tongue came forward, long like his tentacles.

"No," Jaehan rasped, but he was frozen now. Frozen with fear. His voice broke, a little sob escaping him. "Let me go. Let me go."

For a moment, I stopped. For a moment, I was worried that he really wanted this to end.

But he hadn't used his safeword.

"Do you know what to say?" I snarled.

He let out another little sob, shivering in Charlie's tentacles. Charlie had him turned so that his front faced him, his back facing me.

Charlie growled, one that was loud enough to send the birds scattering into the night.

"Yes," Jaehan cried. "I know!"

Good.

I lunged forward, ripping my claws through his clothing. The fabric tore, and Charlie's tentacles moved, one strong one wrapping around his chest under his arms. That left his body exposed and let him struggle more, but he wasn't going anywhere.

Jaehan kicked out, letting out another scream as I pulled his pants and underwear free. Tentacles immediately spread his legs, giving me the perfect access to his ass and cock.

Charlie let out a low laugh. *You're still hard even though you're begging us to stop. Stupid little witch.*

His voice echoed through our minds and I growled, dragging my claws down Jaehan's back.

He cried out, trying to yank free.

"Please! I'm begging you!"

"Your begs mean nothing to monsters," I snarled.

I reached down, gripping my cock as I leaned forward and licked him. I could taste his emotions, his sweat and fear running together.

His fear and arousal.

I drove my tongue into his ass, thrusting it into him. He cried out, his begs becoming louder.

"No! Not there!" Jaehan cried.

I stroked my cock, pleasure working through me as I tasted my mate. His slick, his heat, everything about him told me he wanted to be bred by both of my cocks.

He cried out again as I pulled free. I leaned around and laughed, realizing that Charlie's tongue had wrapped around his cock and was jerking him off.

Jaehan's head tipped back, his cries turning into ones of pleasure. Charlie lowered him down, still holding him spread for me. His ass was at the perfect height, and my cocks were desperate to fill him.

"You're taking both of them," I growled. "Both of them together."

"No," he whispered, but we both knew that really meant yes.

He wanted to feel both of my cocks inside of him. He wanted to know what it would be like to have both of them spread him wide and to be filled with my seed while our other mate jerked his cock.

I gripped my cocks together, rubbing both heads over his ass. He was already slick, his body lubed as much as it could be.

I pushed forward, grunting as I forced both of them inside of him together. He moaned, his body jerking as he took the first inch.

"You're so big," he groaned. "Fuck."

His voice echoed around us, punctuated by the sound of his cock being stroked by Charlie's tongue. More tentacles moved around the two of us, and I gasped as my hand was replaced by a tentacle to hold my cocks together as I eased inside.

Teamwork, Charlie laughed.

"Fuck," I grunted, a low moan combining with Jaehan's.

He felt so fucking good. His voice pitched with more sounds, his body shivering as I gripped his hips and eased in more.

Fuck, he was really taking both of my cocks. I shuddered as a wave of pleasure moved through me, my shadows engulfing us as I thrust more into him.

Every inch, he cried. Every inch, his body took both of my cocks.

I eased back for a moment and then plunged forward again, snarling. My control was starting to slip, my desire growing stronger and stronger.

He was mine. Mine to fuck and breed, to chase and love.

Love? Fuck. Could monsters even love?

Yes, Charlie answered.

Could he hear my questions?

Breed him.

His words egged me on and finally, my control snapped.

I thrust forward, giving Jaehan the rest of both my cocks. He screamed, but then it turned into a cry of intense pleasure as I began to pump in and out of him. I lost myself to the movements, lost myself as I fucked him.

"Just a fucking toy for us monsters," I snarled. "A fucking toy that I'm breeding."

"Please," Jaehan begged. "Fuck! Please don't stop!"

I grinned now, a dark laugh slipping out as I fucked him even harder. I moved back and forth, the sound of our skin slapping together turning me on even more.

All while Charlie stroked him. All while he bound him with his tentacles, his beastly form exposed completely.

I thrust forward even harder, getting closer and closer to cumming.

CHAPTER ELEVEN

tears and fears

CHARLIE

BILLY FUCKED our mate harder and harder, the darkness that came from him growing stronger. He let out short growls and grunts, Jaehan's entire body moving with each pump.

I held him in place, pulling my tongue from his dripping cock. I snaked it up his body, tasting his essence. Tears streamed down his face, his mouth parted in ecstasy.

I forced my tongue between his lips, plunging it down his throat like a tentacle. He choked, his body thrashing and eyes flying open as I used him. His screams became muffled as we used him, Billy and me finding a brutal rhythm.

One of my tentacles wrapped around his cock again, stroking it while a smaller one began to rub over the head. I pulled my tongue free of his mouth, enjoying the sound of him dragging in air.

Mine, I told him. *Say it. I want to hear you say you belong to us, omega.*

"I'm yours," he sobbed, his words broken with pants. "I belong to both of you."

I smiled, satisfied by his words. I then lowered my head watching as my tentacles played with him.

I rubbed the head of his cock with the smallest tendril now, one that might be able to push inside. I pulled his foreskin back, the tendril straightened as the tip pushed into his small hole.

He cried out, a sound of pain. I paused for a moment, looking up at him.

"Don't stop," he panted. "Oh fuck, oh fuck."

I smiled. Being with him had already made me realize a few things about myself.

One being that I liked these noises he made a little too much.

The tentacle moved into him a little bit more, his hips jerking in pain. I was slow, keeping his cock still even as Billy thrust into him. I listened to his breaths, knowing he was close to filling our mate.

I would only tease his cock this way until Billy filled him.

I eased the tentacle into him more, and he cried out. I looked up again, amazed by his face of pleasure and pain. Even in the darkness, I could see the streams of tears.

I slid another tentacle to his mouth. *Bite it if you need to*, I said, offering it to him.

He parted his lips and I moved the tentacle there, chuckling as he bit down hard. It didn't hurt me, instead just making my cock hard despite the fact that I had already filled him several times today.

He groaned as his little teeth held on until he let go, his head tipping back in pleasure.

"I'm going to cum," Billy snarled.

His thrust became faster, his movements harder. I slowly pulled the tentacle free and began to stroke Jaehan's shaft.

I was going to force him to cum.

"I can't again," Jaehan cried. "There's no way."

Of course there was. The way was that his body belonged to me, and I wanted him to cum.

I stroked him faster until he let out a helpless noise.

Billy let out a loud roar, a growl that reverberated through the forest. With one final thrust, he started to cum.

With one final stroke, so did Jaehan.

His cum shot out onto me, his cock jerking. I grinned, licking it up from the tentacles.

The two of them were panting, their breaths harsh. Billy let out a soft moan and I very slowly let go of Jaehan, letting Billy take him into his arms. The two of them sank to the ground, his movements gentle.

The darkness started to recede, and my form began to morph back into my regular one.

I knelt down in front of them, cupping Jaehan's face.

"Hi," he whispered, letting out a little sob.

I leaned down, kissing him. He took it, his arms wrapping around me for a moment.

"I'm taking us to home," Billy grunted. "Hold on to me."

We both held onto him, and a circle of darkness was drawn around us. The three of us fell through a portal, landing on his massive bed. The mattress bounced, the blankets fluffing up.

"Ah," Billy said, looking up at me. "Towel, perhaps, unless we want to sleep in a bed of cum."

I snorted, looking around the room. There was a towel hanging on the door so I grabbed it, sliding it beneath the two of them.

Jaehan let out a little noise and Billy lifted him, slowly pulling his cocks free.

"Oh," Jaehan gasped, his body melting now.

The two of us worked together to get him cleaned up and then I climbed onto the bed. The three of us relaxed, my mind spinning.

That had been...that had been something I would never forget.

"How are you both feeling?" Billy asked, snuggling Jaehan closer between us.

Jaehan held up a thumbs up, letting out a little noise.

I smiled, moving closer to him too. "Good. I want to hear words from our omega though."

"I'm good," Jaehan said. "Fuck. That was a lot. But good."

I nodded.

Billy rubbed him gently, nuzzling him. "You know we love you."

Jaehan was quiet for a moment and then lifted his head, his eyes wide. "Love?"

"Yes," Billy said.

Jaehan looked at me and I nodded.

Love. It was still a funny feeling, one that I wasn't the most familiar with. But it was true.

This wasn't just someone lying next to me that I could forget about. Jaehan wasn't someone that I would simply leave. I cared about him. I cared about Billy.

They were mine.

Jaehan settled back down. He was quiet for a few moments and then my ears perked at the sound of a soft sniffle.

Billy and I were immediately sitting up. I scooped Jaehan up sitting him in my lap.

"I'm okay," he said, but the tears said otherwise.

"Jaehan," Billy said softly. "Are you okay? Too fast?"

"No," he whispered, wiping his face. "No. I just never thought this would happen. I never thought that I would find one person, let alone two. And I...I've wanted this for so long. I've wanted this since I could remember and now that I have it, it's even more than I imagined."

My chest warmed and ached at the same time. His words made me sad, echoing the same feeling that I had since I could remember.

Billy leaned forward, kissing Jaehan's forehead.

"We're here for you," I said. "I know that I am new to this. But I want this more than anything else in this world. And I am happy that we are together. We have a lot of learning to do, a lot of exploring, but we're no longer alone."

Jaehan nodded, smiling. "It's nice."

"It is," Billy agreed. "Now. Let's get some water, have a quick shower, and then sleep. Tomorrow is hump day."

CHAPTER TWELVE

spells

JAEHAN

I DIDN'T WANT Billy to go to work, but he slipped out quickly and quietly before I had the chance to argue.

I was in the nest, sore and sleepy. I wasn't sure what time it was, but I kept falling back asleep and then waking up.

Last night had been a nightmare and a dream. A hellish pleasure that I wanted to experience all over again.

Both Billy and Charlie were monsters. Beings that had hunted me in the forest. I had never run that fast before, and they had still caught me with ease.

I thought back to the feeling of Charlie's tentacle *inside* of my cock. I never thought something like that would feel good. It had stung at first, but then there had been a searing pleasure in knowing that he was inside of me.

Then there were both of Billy's cocks. I'd never taken anything that big before, but it had been worth it.

The two of them were perfect for me.

"Hello," Charlie said, nuzzling me.

We were spooning, his arms wrapped around me. It was warm, the room cool and dark. The curtains were drawn and I liked that we were surrounded by Billy's things.

"Hi," I whispered, closing my eyes again.

"Billy said that there is food for breakfast. I can try to cook something, but I'm not sure what. Whatever you want today, I will make happen."

"Can you make Billy come home?" I asked.

"Aside from that," he said, his voice gentle.

My eyes teared up for a moment and I wasn't even sure why. I knew he had to work, and then in a way he was going so that he could protect us. He wanted to keep up with everything that was going on, but it still hurt my feelings that he wasn't here.

Charlie made a noise. "My love, he will return later today. What else can I do for you?"

"I don't know," I said, palming away a tear. "My emotions are all over the place today."

"That's okay," Charlie said. "It's okay."

I nodded and he turned me over. I buried my face into his chest, breathing in his scent. It was calming, the only thing that could actually calm me right now.

"What if they take him?" I whispered.

"They won't," Charlie said.

"You don't know that," I whispered. "They took me and I'm strong. My magic is strong, Charlie."

"I know it is," he murmured. "I know you are, my love. I've never seen you as weak. I never will."

"I'm worried I just found both of you and everything will get taken away again. What if it happens and I can't help?"

"You aren't alone," Charlie said. "Remember? You have

me. You have the office. Inferna and Art and Calen are good, even though you've just met them. Anne, Alex, Lora, Mich, and Cinder. All of them are good. If something happens to Billy, we won't be alone. You won't be trapped again."

I made a noise, squeezing my eyes shut. "What if I'm too broken now?"

"They never broke you. They hurt you, but you didn't break. You are here now, and you are strong and safe."

I nodded, letting his words comfort me.

He was right. And I had to trust Billy.

He had escaped them before.

"I just wonder why they want us," I said.

"You really can't remember anything?" Charlie asked.

I pressed my lips together, trying to think back. It was like there was a wall around that time, and I could only remember bits and pieces.

"What if...what if you have a spell on you?" Charlie asked.

What if I did?

I frowned, sitting up. Charlie sat up too, his expression concerned.

What if I did? What if I had heard things and just couldn't remember them?

I leaned over the bed, grabbing my phone off the side table. I pulled up my contacts, clicking on the only witch I knew who might be able to help. I hit the call button, listening to the ringing.

I didn't want to involve my mother in this. I didn't want to involve this witch either.

But in a way, she was already involved.

"Hello? Jaehan?" Ember asked, her voice concerned.

"Hey," I said, "are you already at work?"

"Yes," she said. "But it's lunch time. Are you okay?"

I looked at the clock, fighting off a swear. We had really slept in today.

"I need your help," I said. "I know that your magic is healing."

"It is…"

"But would you be able to heal someone who might have a spell on them? A binding one?"

"I might be able to," Ember said. "I mean. Yes. I can. But why? Are you cursed?"

"I think so," I whispered. "I think the whole omega witch group might be. At least our memories. Because none of us can remember right?"

There had been seven of us total who had been hired on to Warts & Claws, and none of us had memories of exactly what had happened.

"Right," she said. "Hmm. Where are you right now?"

"I'm at Billy's with Charlie."

"Who is Charlie?"

"He's an invisible tentacled demon who works at the office and is my mate," I said.

Ember cursed under her breath, sighing. "Damn it, I knew you were going to end up mated."

"It's quite nice," I said, scowling. Charlie chuckled next to me. "You should try it sometime."

Ember snorted. "Find me an orc woman or a vampire and then we'll talk."

I smirked. "Okay, deal. So, can you try it out?"

Ember sighed. "Sure, but when?"

I looked at Charlie, making a face. "I'll be up there soon."

Charlie shook his head, already knowing what I was

going to ask. Before Ember could say another word, I hung up.

"Come on," I said, sliding out of bed.

I started to stand, but my legs wobbled and I sat back down.

"Jaehan, you need rest," Charlie said. "We can try tomorrow morning. This doesn't need to happen now."

"I want to find out," I pleaded.

"You silly witch," Charlie said, sliding across the bed too. "You can't even stand. Can you not rest for today? We will talk with Billy tonight, make plans to make sure you are safe, and then we will meet her. Please."

I sighed, thinking over his words.

"Just... lie back down," he said. "Text Ember and tell her tomorrow morning. We will go into Thursday with a plan. Please."

Charlie saying please wasn't fair. How could I tell him no?

I groaned, leaning back on the bed with a grunt. "Fine. Fine, but only because I love you."

Charlie grinned, one of his tentacles sliding across my thighs. "Love me, hmm?"

I arched a brow, looking up at him. "Yes."

He leaned down, kissing me deeply. I relaxed beneath him, melting into the kiss.

He was right of course.

Waiting until tomorrow morning made sense.

At least then, we could talk to Billy. Maybe then, we could take time to mate.

Charlie stood up, letting out a groan as he stretched. "Text her. I am going to go take a look at the kitchen and see if there is anything I can cook."

"You can look up recipes on your phone," I said, watching as he left the room.

Charlie shook his head, muttering about how everything is on phones now.

I snorted. He was cute when he grumbled.

I opened my phone, sent Ember the text, and then sat up. My muscles were tired, but the heat was still going strong.

I heard Charlie let out a curse from the kitchen.

With a laugh, I slowly stood up and wandered to the kitchen.

Food, snuggles, and tentacle sex until Billy got home sounded like a dream come true.

CHAPTER THIRTEEN

blackmail and blueballs

BILLY

"I'M WORRIED," Inferna said, crossing her arms.

I was sitting in her office with Cinder, Art, and Alex. I didn't know how I felt about sitting in on their meeting, but I was the one who had found the note, so it made sense.

"Why are they after omegas?" Inferna asked, taking a sip of her coffee.

There was a cat bed on the desk with Biscuit, the hairless, ancient, demented cat that had everyone in the room except Inferna on pins and needles.

She turned around, her eyes looking over us and landing on Alex.

Cinder leaned back in their chair, shaking their head. "It has to be because of their magic. There is something about it that they are using somehow, but I'm not sure."

"Alex," Inferna said, her dark eyes narrowing. "Care to contribute?"

Alex arched a brow, meeting her fierce gaze. "You don't have to talk to me like that."

"Oh, yes I do," she said, leaning against the desk.

Biscuit made a clicking noise and Inferna rested her hand on her little body, petting her. The cat stared at Alex, clicking.

"Fuck. Inferna, that thing is a demon," Alex said, shaking his head.

"Yes, well. We're watching her this week while my aunt and uncles are out of town. They're going to Ireland for a dragon-shifter event and it was strictly no pets, as some dragon shifters eat pets apparently. I don't know," she sighed. "She's a great cat and if you piss her off and die, I won't have any remorse."

Art made a face. "Don't piss the cat off, she likes to take revenge."

Inferna snorted. "Off topic. Alex."

Alex sighed and leaned back in his chair, looking up at the ceiling. "There might be some things I have left out. But it's because I'm still getting a handle on what is happening."

We all stared at him. He looked back around, grimacing.

"I am a witch as you all know," Alex said. "And I am also an omega."

"Fucking gods," Art said, standing up from his chair. He went to the window, his hands on his hips.

Cinder shook their head, glaring. "Seriously?"

"I was the first omega," Alex said, arching a brow.

I squinted at him, shaking my head. My perception of the witch who had stepped out of a portal and zapped a vampire and witch to dust was infinitely different now seeing him sitting across from me, telling us information that would have been good to know from the beginning.

Inferna let out a frustrated breath. "Alex, I swear to the gods."

Alex held up his hands, making a face. "Some of the things I have withheld were things that had to be. For your safety. That's part of being the boss, Inferna. As you know."

"This isn't about being the boss," Inferna said. "And you know that. I just wish we would have had this information. Because every time we find something out, you have a little more to tell us and it makes me doubt you. It makes all of us doubt you."

Alex was silent for a moment and then he pressed his lips together, looking away. "It's complicated."

"Is he your lover?" I asked.

Alex snorted, shaking his head. "No. I wish that were the case, it would be a lot more poetic. Alfred is... was my best friend. And I think there were romantic feelings from him for me that I did not reciprocate. And then my first heat happened and it changed things. It was confusing because I was just a witch, but he knew what it was. He's a werewolf, after all. It didn't happen until much later in life, but when it did, our friendship changed. Slowly we started to hate each other. And then the company we built together slowly became a way for him to fight me. But...I didn't know he was hurting others."

Alex's eyes darkened. I glanced around the room and then back at him, studying him. He had black hair with a bolt of white, a beard that was very well kept, and he was always in a nice suit. He also liked to wear gloves. Every morning when he came in, he always had them on. When he left for the day, he wore them as well. His eyes were the same color as the bolts of lightning I'd seen come out of those gloved fingers, a striking blue.

"It was a game of cat and mouse to me, but it was much

more to him," Alex said. "The reason they are targeting this office is because of me. Omegas, in general, are rare. And yet, we've encountered a dozen or so in the last few weeks. This is my fault. It is a curse, one that will never be lifted. Other omegas flock to me. The unmated ones. The witches who ended up with the same curse, or blessing depending on how you see it."

Cinder stood up now, glaring down at Alex. "So, leave."

"I can't, Cinder," Alex said. "Not now. Now that they are here, they are obviously in danger. And while you and Art are powerful witches, you are not as old as I am. You are not as well versed in the laws of magic or the thousands of spells that we have. I can reduce a soul to dust. Can you? No."

"No, but I can fucking fight," Cinder said, still glaring. "We all can. We did just fine the day I was taken."

"Well, you had a very powerful demon at your side," Alex said, looking at me.

I shook my head, letting out a frustrated breath. "They will come for us," I said. "And what will we do? How will we protect our mates? How will we protect those who work here? The witches have already been through enough. They've felt enough pain. It's not fair to leave them defenseless and without a plan."

"Which is why I am staying," Alex said. "I understand that all of you are angry."

"Angry is an understatement," Inferna said, taking a sip of her coffee. "If there is anything else, you need to tell us now. Or I will be calling my godfather and he will take you out, and I will not feel a shred of guilt about it."

Alex rolled his eyes, but this Biscuit clicked again, the noise echoing through the office.

"Biscuit has offered to eat you," Inferna said, smirking over the rim of her mug.

Alex stared at the cat for a moment and then shook his head. "The only other thing I can think of— this office will get worse before it gets better."

"We need to warn everyone," Cinder said.

"But if we do, then our enemy knows," Alex said. "And some of the employees here are definitely enemies. I just don't know who yet."

"I'm bringing my friend in," Inferna said, setting her mug down. "To help with that. She is a vampire named Minni. I am also bringing in another friend, the daughter of an orc friend of the family. Her name is Lea. Both of them are dear to me, and both of them will act as undercover agents for us. They will help weed out the enemies."

"An orc as undercover?" Alex asked, arching a brow.

Inferna raised a brow right back, her tail flicking behind her. "Really, I don't think doubting me right now is the best move for you, boss. She's learned from the best."

Alex shook his head, but didn't argue. "Sometimes I wonder about your family."

Inferna snorted. "Very large, very diverse, and very lethal. We've got creatures of all kinds and humans too. And it's very strong," she said.

Alex nodded, giving a little smile. "It's good to have that. Good family is nice."

I felt the sting of that statement, knowing what he meant. I had never thought about it too much, but the idea of having such a network of people who loved and cared sounded.... like a fairytale.

But, I had thought that about falling in love once upon a time too. Maybe happy endings weren't reserved for the books.

I felt my phone in my pocket go off and I reached in, pulling it out. I stole a glance at the text message, trying not to show my full screen to the room in case Jaehan or Charlie had sent pictures or video again.

Fuck, they'd nearly killed me yesterday.

It was a photo again, but this time it was just of the two of them snuggling. I let out a little sigh, wishing I were there.

But I needed to be here right now in case something happened.

Another text came through from Jaehan and I read it, frowning.

JAEHAN: Tomorrow I need to go into the office and meet up with Ember to try and lift a spell that I think is locking my memories. She is a healing witch and would be able to help.

I reread that a few times, thinking it over.

"Question," I said, frowning. I slipped my phone back in my pocket and then looked up at everyone. "If Jaehan has a spell on him to block his memories of what happened, what would be the best way to undo it?"

Art turned to look at me, followed by Cinder and Alex. Inferna tilted her head, thinking it over.

"Well," Alex said. "You would need someone who is very good with healing magic and with puzzles. Witches who cast such spells are notorious for being tricky. It is like walking through a jungle without a guide, and there are traps meant to hurt the one attempting to heal. But...what makes you think that is the case?"

"I mean, it makes sense," Cinder said, interrupting.

"None of the omegas can remember what happened to them exactly. Even my sister, when she was initially taken. Before I bargained my life away to save her from your evil friend."

The coffee wasn't the only thing that was bitter this morning, but I couldn't blame them. All of us were angry and tired of fighting.

"Not my friend anymore," Alex muttered.

"Jaehan says that Ember is a healing witch," I said. "And that he wants to come in tomorrow morning to try and have her lift the spell, if there is one."

"Fuck no," Cinder said. "I don't want Ember getting involved in anything."

"If she can help, then she can help," I said, scowling.

"He shouldn't come into the office," Inferna said firmly. "It's not safe at this point. I don't know why Poppins felt the need to send us a warning, and if anything, it could have been to fuck with us more. But, regardless, the safest place for him right now is at your home. It seems like you are the target right now, which makes sense, considering you escaped them like it was nothing. And Cinder was fired, so I think that means they are safe."

"If all of us are here on standby, I think it will be okay," I said. "But I mean all of us. Even the lightning witch," I said, looking at Alex.

Alex nodded, looking at me directly. "I will be here, Billy."

"It's concerning that they would have them spelled," Art said. "And perhaps it is for a reason. I don't like the idea of unlocking memories that could be damaging. Sometimes ignorance is bliss."

"Ignorance is bliss," Inferna said, "but I'd rather know I'm in hell instead of thinking I'm in heaven. And even if there is a spell on them locking these memories, they will still have emotions and changes in behavior that reflect what happened. But they won't be able to know why."

"I don't like this," Cinder said, shaking their head. "Ember—"

"Can make decisions for herself," I said, meeting their violet gaze.

Art sighed, crossing his arms. He came around the desk, leaning against it next to Inferna. She bumped his shoulder, giving him a playful smile.

"So tomorrow morning," Cinder said, looking at me. "You will bring your mates, and we will all be ready in case something happens. Ember can attempt to undo the potential spell, or at least see if it exists."

"Yes," I said. "Yes. That's what we will do. And maybe she can see if Charlie has a spell on him as well."

"You think he does?" Cinder asked.

Art surprised me by being the one to nod. "I think he does. I know that I can't see him, but I have never met a creature that was invisible that wasn't a ghost or spirit. I know we don't know all creatures in existence, and with enough lineage, anything can happen— but... it seems unnatural in his case."

"He also can't remember some things," I said, standing up. "Can't remember what happened more than a century ago. I've been around for a few hundred years, and while some things fall through the cracks, I still remember everything."

Inferna nodded. "I realize that I am quite young, but my father is ancient and he has said the same thing. In fact, many of the creatures I know that are old still remember."

"You remember phases," I chuckled.

Like the phase where I had emerged from hell and done a lot of damage to a human village.

Or the phase where I liked to mess with priests.

Or the phase where I had been on the wrong side of a battle between monsters and humans.

I had learned a lot. I had changed a lot. And the one thing I found was that forgiveness took time, but it could still happen. Even years later.

And now this was my work in an office phase, one that was becoming more and more interesting. Charlie and Jaehan were now part of my life, and would be until the end of my time.

"Things change when you find love," I said softly.

Everyone but Alex nodded.

My phone went off in my pocket again and I pulled it out.

I immediately regretted it, desire burning through me.

"Fucking hell," I sighed.

"I don't want to know," Alex said, holding up a hand.

"No you don't," I snorted, walking towards the door. "If you'll excuse me, I think our meeting is done."

Inferna smirked. "Indeed. Have fun with whatever picture that was."

I fought the urge to hiss at my boss and quietly slipped out of the room, cursing under my breath. I looked at the photo again, sucking in a breath.

My cocks started to harden, all the blood threatening to leave my body and just rush there. My balls ached, the need to fill Charlie and Jaehan making me curse again.

Charlie had sent a very provocative photo, and for that — I was going to make sure it was his turn tonight.

CHAPTER FOURTEEN

mating

CHARLIE

I KNEW SENDING the photo to Billy would both arouse him and piss him off since he was still at work. So, I wasn't surprised that by the time he got home— he was ready to do something more than cuddle.

The door to the house opened and I looked up from where I sat. Jaehan was in the bath, taking one with Epsom salts that would soothe his muscles.

Billy shut the door behind him and crossed the room in a few direct strides. My stomach flipped as he came up to me, dragging me from my seat and shoving me against the wall.

"Hi," I rasped.

"You're a fucking brat," he growled, his eyes dark and wicked. "Sending me a picture of your virgin ass while I was *in a meeting.*"

I fought off a laugh, still holding his gaze. "Maybe I wanted to make you hard while you were in the meeting."

"You would want that," he hissed, his grip on me tightening. "Where is our omega?"

"Taking a bath," I said, smirking.

Billy grabbed me and yanked me through his house, straight to the bedroom. He was rough, shoving me back onto the bed with a growl.

"So impatient," I said, still grinning at him.

His eyes darkened more, another growl leaving him. "I'm going to fucking breed you the same way I bred him if you keep this up, you little bastard."

I liked this side of him. This feisty and dominant side. He didn't need to be careful with me, didn't need to fight the part of him that wanted to throw me across the room.

My cock started to harden and I tilted my head. "As if you could. You're just a fucking demon. You're not stronger than me, even if you want to be," I said. "I have tentacles and what do you have? Darkness?"

That did it. Billy's clothes shed away as he shifted in front of me, letting out his monstrous form. Darkness spread through the room and I heard a quiet mewl.

We both looked up at the doorway to the bathroom where Jaehan stood, his eyes wide.

"Oh, don't worry," I said, grinning at him. "Don't worry, little omega. The monsters can be rough. I want this, to see what he can do."

"You can watch," Billy growled, looking at him.

Jaehan nodded, his eyes still wide. "Okay," he said, finally smiling. "Pretend like I'm not here. This is hot."

I was about to say another snide comment, when a wall of darkness sent me across the room. I hit the floor with a gasp, my breath knocked out of me.

I could feel him coming. I sat up, my tentacles shooting

out just as Billy pounced on me. I rolled out of his grip with a growl, shoving him back.

He let out a low laugh, one of a hunter who had narrowly missed their prey.

"You won't escape me," he said. "I'm fucking you. I'm going to fucking breed you and you're going to regret being such a little brat."

"If you can catch me," I said, rolling to my feet.

Billy lunged towards me, and I used my tentacles to knock his feet from beneath him. He would have hit the floor, but instead— a wave of darkness tore my grip free and I was slammed back onto the bed.

His claws curled around my ankle and he yanked me over, forcing me onto my stomach. I kicked back, a little bit of surprise making me yelp and he climbed on top of me and pinned me down.

I let my tentacles go wild, wrapping them around him as his arm came around my neck in a lock. He pulled back, cutting off my air.

I dragged in a breath as my vision started to darken. I could feel his hard cocks against my ass, but I could also feel his muscles in my tentacled grip.

He thrust his hips against me, his grip easing enough to allow me to breathe. I dragged in air with a moan and felt his claws rip into my clothes. The fabric was torn from me, my skin now bare.

"Fucking monster," he growled. "You may have tentacles but you want this as much as I do. You're not going to fight me," he said, lowering his mouth to my ear. "Are you?"

"No," I rasped, thrusting my ass back against him.

Billy's hold on me didn't lessen, but he did kiss me. Gently. Softly.

Fuck.

I was so hard now, my cock throbbing. Billy kissed me again and then bared his sharp teeth, dragging the tips over my flesh.

Ever since the thought of mating had come up earlier today, it was all I could think about. I wanted him to not only fuck me, but to mate me too. I wanted to make a bond with him, to tie our souls together.

"Mate me," I whispered. "Please."

Billy froze for a moment and then leaned his face back down next to mine. "Mate you? Bond you?"

"Yes," I said. "I want this."

Billy made a noise, a growl of surprise and of... want?

"Fine, you needy little bastard," he said, easing back.

Excitement ran through me. I groaned as he dragged his claws down me, following the places where my tentacles grew from my back.

"Get the lube," Billy said to Jaehan.

I heard the sound of our omega moving, going to a set of drawers that had what we needed. Jaehan came to the bed and Billy took it from him, and then pulled him onto the bed in front of me.

"I said you can watch," Billy said. "So fucking watch."

"Yes, Sir," Jaehan whispered.

I felt Billy's cocks throb against me. I smiled to myself. "Sir? You like being called Sir?"

Billy growled, shoving my head back down into the blankets. "Shut the fuck up."

"Yes, Sir," I mimicked.

That earned me a swat on the ass, the sound echoing through the room.

Billy hissed as he poured lube on my ass, using the head of one of his cocks to rub it in. I sucked in a breath, pleasure burning through me.

He was going to fuck me. He was going to breed me. He was going to bond me.

Fuck.

"Sir," I said, this time my voice a little shaky.

"Don't worry," he said, "It won't hurt too badly."

"Liar," I hissed, but I grinned.

A moan left me as he began to circle my ass with his thumb, easing it in and out. It felt different, unlike anything I had ever experienced before. I sucked in a breath as he pushed his thumb in more, my cock throbbing beneath me.

He still had me pinned to the bed, my legs trapped under his body. I groaned as he began to tease me, warming me up for his cock.

"Please," I whispered.

"Oh? Was that a beg, dear monster?"

Fuck. Was it? I had never begged anyone for anything in my time, I was too proud to do so. But, that had definitely been a plea.

I could smell Jaehan's hormones, his arousal making mine so much more intense. I moved my head so I could look at him on the bed. He was sitting and watching, his eyes glued on our mate's cocks while he stroked his own.

Fuck. "*Please*," I said again.

"You want my monster cock in your virgin ass?"

"Yes," I gasped, my eyes fluttering for a moment.

"So innocent," he chuckled. "Never been fucked like this and now you're begging a monster to pop your cherry and to mate you. How long have you dreamed about this?"

"Fuck you," I said, turning so I could glare at him.

Billy leaned forward and shoved my head back in the blankets, snarling into my ear. "No, I'm going to fuck *you*. Now answer my god damned question. Now."

"No," I said, squirming against him.

He growled, shoving me harder. He replaced his fingers with the head of his cock, and my eyes widened as I realized just how big he was.

"Has nothing ever been in here?"

"No," I whispered.

"Not even one of your tentacles?"

"No," I said, grunting.

Fuck. I had never thought about that. I had used my tentacles to jerk off my cock before, but I had never thought about doing anything else with them.

"Your ass is mine," Billy said. "Say it."

"No," I growled.

He slapped my right cheek, his claws catching my skin. I groaned as pain burst through me, but it was followed by a wave of euphoria.

Fuck, did I like pain?

"Fucking say it."

"My ass is yours," I groaned. "Fuck you, Billy."

Billy spread my ass, his claws digging in my skin as he pushed the head of his cock against me again. I gasped as I felt it force me apart, the head easing inside of me.

My muscles worked hard, stretching around him to accommodate. I let out a pant, a small cry leaving me as he stopped, allowing my body to acclimate.

"Sir," I groaned, this time meaning it.

I had never submitted to anyone in this way. I had never given in like this, never allowed someone to use me the same way that I had used Jaehan today.

How many times had I fucked him today, and yet... now I wanted to be the one bent over and begging.

"Please," I said, pushing back.

I took more of his cock, a low moan leaving me. The

feeling of stretching and taking him was both a little painful and entirely too pleasurable.

"Good boy," he murmured, his voice soothing me in a way I hadn't expected.

"You feel so good," I said, shivering.

"Good," he said, his tone more gentle now.

It was like he was coaxing my body to take him, talking me into taking every fucking inch of his massive cock.

"I don't know how you did both," I gasped, looking up at Jaehan.

He grinned a little, his cheeks flushed and cock hard in his grip. "Practice," he said, letting out a little moan.

"Practice," Billy chuckled. "Practice and his heat. Do you like watching your mates together, little omega?"

"Yes," Jaehan moaned, his breath hitching.

"You like watching me breed him?"

"Yes."

Fuck. A shiver worked through me again as I took more of his cock.

"Still eight more inches to go," Billy said, laughing.

"Eight?!" I gasped.

Fucking hell. I already felt like I was completely filled.

I groaned as he gave a little shove, giving me another inch.

"You're gonna take every inch," he said. "Every fucking one."

I nodded, my body shivering again. Billy gripped my hips, his talons digging into me. I could feel the pain and the pleasure and everything in between, a glorious dance of lust.

I nodded and thrust my hips forward, grinding into the blankets. My cock was so hard and aching now, the desperation to cum starting to build.

"You're not going to cum until I let you," he said, slapping my ass. "You think I'm going to let you cum when you can't even take my entire cock? Fucking bastard."

Fuck. I groaned, shaking my head as he stilled my hips, forcing me not to move even though I was so horny. I was so turned on and it almost hurt not to be able to touch my cock.

"Take every inch like a good boy and then I will allow you to cum. And maybe that will teach you a lesson about being such a fucking brat."

If the lesson was getting fucked like this, then I would be a brat forever.

Jaehan let out a groan, the sound of him pumping his cock filling the room. Billy gave another thrust, forcing more of his cock into me before he pulled out. I cried out as he pumped forward again, giving me even more. The motion made me gasp, my muscles tensing up.

"Relax," Billy hissed. "If you don't relax, you will make this worse for you."

I took in a deep breath, trying to force my muscles to listen. Billy dragged his claws down my back again before pulling out and thrusting back in.

Fuck. The ridges of his cock ran through me, the feeling making my cock leak with precum. How was I supposed to wait to cum when this felt so goddamn good?

"Please," I said. "Please, I want to cum."

"No," he growled. "You still have to take another three inches."

I started to push up onto all fours, but he slammed me back down with a snarl.

"Move again without my permission, and I will stop being gentle. Do you understand?"

"Yes, Sir," I whispered, trembling.

This was both heaven and hell, torture and ecstasy. Billy began to pump into me, his cock dragging in and out of me. Every time he pumped back in, he gave me a little more of his shaft, spreading me a little wider and deeper than before.

I cried out now, the feeling of being impaled like this rushing over me. The sound of Jaehan still stroking made me even more desperate to cum, but I knew the only way that was going to happen now was if I took all of Billy's cock.

I gasped and groaned, the noises I made mirroring the ones that Jaehan had made last night. I had enjoyed listening to them, but now I was starting to lose myself to making them.

It felt good to let go. It felt good to let Billy fuck me how he wanted, to give myself to this breeding.

"Please," I begged. "Please, Sir. Please."

Billy grunted, his movements starting to become faster. He fucked me, his cock thrusting in and out of me at a more brutal pace.

Finally, the last thrust— I felt all of his cock inside of me, his balls slapping against mine. I cried out, never having felt something like this before in my entire life.

"You're so deep," I whimpered. "You're so deep inside of me."

He kept his cock there for a moment, leaning down so he could whisper in my ear. "You're doing so good," he murmured. "You're taking my cock so well for your first time. I'm so proud of you."

The praise made my eyes water, my body pulsing with pleasure.

"Thank you," I whispered.

"I'm going to reward you," he breathed, a growl leaving

him. "Do you want your reward? Are you willing to work for it?"

"Yes," I said, looking up at him.

I held his gaze for a moment, staring into his six eyes. He was my master in this moment and whatever he wanted, I would give.

A slow, fanged grin broke out across his face. His teeth gleamed, ominous and sexy.

He leaned back and planted his hands on my ass cheeks. He began to thrust, his movements harder and faster. I screamed as he began to fuck me exactly how he wanted, taking every inch of his cock over and over again.

My thoughts became jumbled in my mind, every last one leaving me. All I knew was I was his to use, mated to a demon of darkness. His balls slapped against mine, all of this echoed by our mate's own pleasure.

"When I cum, I want you to cum on his face, Jaehan," Billy gasped. "Do you understand me?"

"Yes," Jaehan cried. "Fuck."

"And when I say now, you're going to cum too," he growled at me.

I nodded, my words soft grunts. My mind began to float, my body bathed in pleasure as he thrust faster.

"Fuck, I'm getting close," he grunted.

Fuck. I panted as I took him, listening to both of their cries. I was so close, so fucking close. I needed to cum—could barely hold it—

"Now!"

I gasped as I started to cum, shooting hot seed from the head of my cock.

Jaehan moved closer and I looked up, watching as he started to cum too. I closed my eyes with a moan as his seed shot onto my face, all while Billy began to fill me. Warmth burned into me as his cum pumped inside me, a groan of pleasure leaving all of us.

Jaehan panted and sat back, his chest heaving. I opened my eyes, swiping my tongue over my lips where his cum had landed.

Fuck.

Billy leaned forward, kissing up my spine. I moaned as he dragged his tongue up my spine, pausing to kiss each tentacle. I gasped as his teeth scraped my skin, his cock still buried inside of me.

"Where do you want it?" He murmured.

"Anywhere you want," I grunted, my eyes watering.

His touch became gentler, his lips leaving kisses.

"I love you," he whispered. "I love you already. For everything that you are."

"Thank you," I said. "I... I love you too."

I couldn't stop it now. A tear rolled down my cheek, my mind still spinning. I heard Jaehan sniffle, his hand resting on my head.

Billy let out a soft hum and kissed his way up to the back of my neck. He swept my hair to the side and leaned in, his teeth piercing against the tendon.

I closed my eyes, letting the moment truly sink in.

This was where the loneliness ended. This was where my new life would begin. One where I wasn't an invisible monster lurking in the shadows. One where I had two people who could see me, who cared.

"I love you," Billy whispered again. "So much. And you're mine, little monster."

I nodded, choking on my words. I didn't know what to say, but I could feel everything. I could feel the weight lifting off my chest, the feeling that I was unworthy melting like snow in the sun.

His teeth sank into my skin and I grunted, feeling the snap of our bond coming to life. I gasped as I felt our souls tie, my blood filling his mouth. He groaned, drinking from me before sliding his hand forward, offering me his wrist.

I took it, immediately piercing him with my teeth. His blood tasted dark and rich, reminding me of bourbon and the forest. I drank from him, a growl leaving me as we sealed our mating bond.

He slowly pulled back and so did I.

"Jaehan, love," he said, "Get a towel."

Jaehan hopped up from the bed, coming back with a towel. Billy slipped it underneath us.

He held me for a moment and then slowly sat back, pulling his cock free of me.

His cum began to drip from me and I groaned, melting into the bed.

Fuck.

My blood rushed in my head, in my veins. My head spun as the feelings of everything that had just happened settled in.

Billy rolled over to one side, Jaehan taking the other. Both of them holding me tight.

I liked having Jaehan between us, but in this moment... being in the middle was something I couldn't complain about.

CHAPTER FIFTEEN
bonded

JAEHAN

WATCHING the two of them mate had been one of the most beautiful, sexy, and carnal things I had ever seen. I had thought that last night in the forest would be the epitome of me being turned on, but the intimacy of mating was something that couldn't be beat.

The three of us were cuddled in bed now, clean and fed and resting. It was still early in the night since Billy had come home and gone straight to Charlie.

I smiled a little.

I was happy. I was beyond happy. And I knew that soon, I would share the same bond that they did now, but I was happy to have been able to witness it.

There was a feeling of compersion, of happiness that they had done this. It had been beautiful.

Charlie let out a soft snore, sliding into sleep. Billy chuckled, his hand moving over our mate to settle on me.

"Hi," I murmured.

"Hi, baby," he said softly. "Are you okay?"

"More than," I said. "More than okay. That was...amazing."

"It was," Billy murmured. "I want to mate you too."

"I know," I said, grinning.

Billy smiled, giving me a soft squeeze. "Sleep. Tomorrow morning we will have some fun before work. And we at least have a plan for the spell."

"Do we?" I asked.

"Yes," he said. "I'll tell you tomorrow, love. Go to bed."

I nodded and closed my eyes. Within a few minutes, I was falling asleep.

THE NEXT MORNING, I woke up with a hard cock pressed against me. I kept my eyes closed, pretending to still sleep as a tentacle slowly moved up my body.

It was hard to fight off a groan, but I did my best. Still, my cock began to harden, and Charlie's exploring tentacle found it. It wrapped around my shaft, tugging it gently while another flicked across one of my nipples.

Fuck. Morning sex was my favorite, and waking up to tentacles exploring me was a dream come true. My breath hitched and I heard a dark chuckle.

"Good morning."

"Morning," I rasped.

The tentacles immediately swept me closer, his cock throbbing against me.

"You could have woken me up with that inside me," I said, smirking.

"Mmm....but then I wouldn't get to hear your morning voice," Charlie teased. "Plus...by the time Billy comes back with breakfast I will be inside of you."

I nodded, my cock now fully hard. I pushed my hips back, grinding against his cock as he began to explore me more with his tentacles. I groaned sleepily, relaxing against him.

Fuck, everything felt so good.

"We're going to mate you," Charlie whispered. "If you are ready."

"Yes," I breathed. "Please. I want this."

"We still have a couple hours before work," he murmured, kissing my shoulder and then neck. "Plenty of time to fuck and mate you before we go to the office."

"I want everyone to know I'm yours," I said.

"Oh they will," Charlie said, his tentacle still stroking my cock.

I gasped, everything feeling good. It was hard not to succumb completely, but why would I stop myself?

Charlie held me still, his hand slipping down between us and helping the head of his cock against my ass. I sucked in a breath as he began to ease in, my groan soft.

It still felt like a dream, still felt like I was waking up. I closed my eyes, allowing the pleasure to wash over me completely. His cock was thick and hard, the ridges and suckers making me gasp.

"Charlie," I whispered. "Fuck, you feel so good."

"I know," he said. "I know now what it's like and it feels fucking good."

Heat rushed through me, that fever of need returning with a vengeance. He held me tight as he began to thrust, humping into me while his tentacles explored me. My nipples ached, tender to the touch. My cock pulsed, begging for him to keep jerking me.

Everything about this moment was perfect.

I groaned as he began to fuck me harder. I heard movement in the room and my eyes opened, my head lifting.

Billy walked into the bedroom, already smiling. He
arched a brow as I cried out, watching the two of us fuck.

He came to the bed, holding up his phone and taking a
picture.

"For later," he said, smirking. "Oh, you look so good
with his cock inside you."

Fuck.

I groaned louder now, unashamed. I was fully awake
with a tentacle cock inside of me, my cock being teased.

Billy took another picture and then put his phone on
the side table. He peeled his clothes off and then shifted
completely, his double cocks hard and dripping.

He climbed onto the bed as Charlie kept fucking me,
offering me his cocks.

I was hungry to taste him and immediately reached up,
sucking the head of his bottom shaft. He grunted and
moved closer, forcing it more into my mouth until he hit the
back of my throat.

I groaned, my cry muffled as he reached down and
gripped my hair.

The two of them worked in a rhythm now, fucking my
throat and ass together. Charlie groaned as he took me, his
breath turning into pants.

"Fuck, I'm getting close."

"Me too," Billy said. "I'm too turned on right now, I
won't last long."

I grunted as they took me, my eyes closing as I sank into
the ecstasy of it. Their movements became quicker and I
found my fingers digging into Billy's thighs as they each
gave a final thrust, filling me with their cum.

I swallowed quickly, moaning as it filled my mouth.

Charlie's cum began to make me feel like I was floating on the clouds again, my entire body thrumming with energy.

Billy pulled his cock free and leaned down, whispering in my ear. "Are you ready?"

"Yes," I rasped. "Please."

He nodded, his lips kissing my forehead. In one swift motion, Charlie lifted me and seated me between the two of them, his cock still inside of me.

Billy kissed one side of my neck while Charlie kissed the other, and then I felt the prick of their fangs.

I gasped as they both sank their teeth into me, crying out at the flash of pain. The spell that I knew, the one that would seal the three of us together, tumbled from my lips as they tasted my blood— our souls becoming one.

The pain of the bite was replaced with absolute euphoria. I melted against the two of them as they drank, their tongues coaxing the blood out as they sucked.

Fuck.

Fuck this was heaven.

I drew in soft breaths as they finished, both of them licking the bites they had made. They pulled back and Charlie rested his chin on my shoulder, Billy pressing his forehead to mine.

"Mates," I whispered. "My mates."

For the first time this week, I could feel the harsh edge of my heat receding. I had more clarity than I ever had before, a sense of rightness.

This was the power of fate.

After all of the nightmares I had lived through recently, this was the dream I had been chasing. The one that had kept my hope alive.

"I love you," Billy said, his voice soft and comforting.

"I love you as well," Charlie murmured.

I nodded, tears filling my eyes. "I love you both. This is...this is more than I ever could have asked for."

"I'm glad this week has gone to hell," Billy chuckled. "The trouble brought me to both of you, so I think it's worth it."

It was true. It was worth it.

"I think...I think we can rest for another half hour and still have time for breakfast and to get ready," Billy said.

"Okay," I smiled. "And tomorrow is Friday too. We're getting closer to the weekend."

"Yes," Charlie said. "And meeting your family."

I smiled at the thought, knowing they would both be welcome.

The three of us sank back into bed, stealing the last bit of time before we had to go into work and face the rest of the world.

CHAPTER SIXTEEN
thursday spells

BILLY

I DIDN'T LIKE the thought of a witch getting into Jaehan's mind, even if it was someone we could trust.

Our whole group stood in the shifting room, the doors locked and all of us ready. Ready for what, we weren't entirely sure.

Mich, Anne, and Lora were all outside— keeping an eye on the door and on anything suspicious.

Inferna, Calen, Art, Cinder, Alex, Ember, Jaehan, Charlie, and I were all in the shifting room in a circle. Ember and Jaehan were in the middle, their nerves making me nervous.

Ember could be trusted, that we all knew. She was Cinder's sister and had already seen her fair share of shit. She's already faced her own battles and was well aware of how fierce the enemies were.

Her long purple hair was tied up into a bun, her brows

drawn together. She and Jaehan stared at each other, almost oblivious to the rest of us.

I could feel him through our bonds. I could feel all of his concerns, all of his worry, but also the hint of...hope.

Hope that somewhere inside of him, the answers to this looming puzzle would be found. More information would bring us closer to understanding why this bastard did what he did, and why everything was happening.

All of the revelations from Alex had left me feeling numb in a way, but it was moments like this that I knew he wasn't the bad guy. He watched Jaehan and Ember with the same apprehension and concern that I did.

All of us were ready for something to go wrong, and yet.... What would I be able to do if it did?

It wasn't like me to feel fear. My entire life I had used others' fears against them, and this was poetic and terrible to have it thrown back on me like this.

"We will figure it out," Ember said, looking at Jaehan. "If you're spelled, even if I can't undo it, we will find someone who can."

"If you feel like you are in danger, you need to come back out," Cinder said, obviously concerned. They watched their sister with a look of dread, of worry.

I wasn't a witch, I was a demon, therefore my knowledge of how their magic worked was limited. I knew that magic could be dark, could be poisonous, and could be deadly.

"Seriously," Art said, his voice stern. "The moment something feels off, retreat. We can't afford to have either one of you hurt."

"Yeah, there's no workers' comp for this," Alex teased, trying to lighten the mood.

His words, if anything, made the situation more grave.

Inferna let out a hiss, giving him a dark look. One that said to shut the fuck up.

I refocused on Ember and Jaehan. One wrong move, and both she and Jaehan could be hurt.

But...he was bonded to Charlie and me now. I had to keep that thought in my mind, the reminder that the three of us were tied together, which meant I could feel more of him. His soul was like a neighbor's window at night, the curtains drawn back, and I could see enough to know if he needed me.

"We are here," Calen said, giving her a gentle nod. "You have three other witches in the room. You aren't alone."

Ember nodded, squaring her shoulders as she held out her hands.

Jaehan hesitated for a moment and then took them. Charlie moved next to me, edging a little closer.

He was worried. But just like me, he was using the bonds to keep him from stopping our mate. He was using this little bit of hope to keep him from jumping in, just like I wanted to.

Ember closed her eyes. Her lips parted on the faintest whisper, the air becoming balmy. Her skin started to glow with inner sunshine that made me want to turn away.

My eyes widened as Jaehan did too, taking on the same golden hue as the healing witch. They became harder to look at as she began to hum a spell, her voice melodic.

My stomach twisted, nerves working through me. We all stared at them, watching for anything that could go wrong.

Ember continued to speak the incantation, her words turning into something that reminded me of a spring breeze. Her words had a lilt, the golden hue shimmering.

She was like sunshine and a field of flowers, which

made me want to hiss. I was a demon after all, and being in the presence of someone whose magic was so gentle made me want to turn away.

Alex crossed his arms, his face twisting in concentration.

My heart began to hammer a little faster and I closed my eyes. I could feel my bond with Jaehan tugging harder, and a wave of concern washed over me.

I felt another painful tug, one that wasn't from Jaehan but from...

My eyes flew open and I turned, seeing Charlie's knees buckle. I lunged forward, catching him before he hit the floor.

"Fuck!" I snarled.

The others started to move towards me, but I realized they couldn't see him. How the fuck were they going to help?

"What's happening?" Calen asked, coming closer.

Charlie let out a ragged groan, hunching over.

"Charlie?!" I asked, shaking him. "Charlie, what's wrong?"

He looked up at me and I gasped as his rainbow eyes turned black. They widened with terror as the colors were engulfed, the darkness spreading. Consuming.

He parted his lips, inky black blood spilling forward.

Horror filled me unlike anything I had ever felt in my life. Ember's voice continued to rise and I let out a cry.

"Stop her! Stop them! This is hurting Charlie!"

Cinder lunged forward, stepping into the circle of magic to pull them apart. The room immediately rumbled and Charlie screamed, his tentacles writhing as if he were choking.

Fuck. FUCK. Panic filled me and I looked up, shocked to see everyone trying to pull Jaehan and Ember apart.

There was no stopping them now. It was as if their hands were glued together, the spell going on and on.

In all of my time, I had never seen anything like this.

"Charlie," I cried, shaking him.

I held him in my arms as he trembled and writhed, holding him as he twisted in pain.

More black blood spilled from his mouth, hitting the floor. He threw it up, his entire body wrenching. His tentacles began to darken, his opal skin taking on a gray hue.

Fuck.

I had to do something.

My heart pounded in my chest as I let go of him, rising to my feet.

I lifted my hands, calling on my own demonic magic. Calling on the circles of hell, on the fire and brimstone I had kept at bay for so long.

Ember let out a scream as darkness filled the room, bursting from my body and rushing over her magic.

It was a fight. It was fight that I didn't want to win anymore, to devour light with darkness. But I had no choice. I had to stop whatever was happening.

I screamed, my six eyes filled with tears as I gave it everything I had.

The golden glow was overtaken, her cry echoing out.

She let go, immediately collapsing into Cinder, Alex, and Inferna's arms.

Jaehan collapsed too, caught by Calen and Art.

My knees buckled and I landed in a puddle of the black blood. I looked over at Charlie, panting from the amount of energy I had just given.

He raised his head for a moment and then fell to the side, his eyes falling closed.

Fuck.

I felt hollow. I felt empty.

Fear curled up, an unfriendly emotion. The type that threatened to drag me down and hold me there until I drowned in it.

The door to the shifting room burst open and Mich came through, his eyes wide as Lora squeezed past. They ran to us, but no one could see Charlie.

I crawled to him, my gaze torn between him and Jaehan. I didn't know who to go to, who to help.

"Jaehan is okay," Art said, giving me a concerned look. "Focus on Charlie. We can't help him because we can't see him."

I nodded, letting out a broken breath.

Surely both of them were going to be okay.

Surely I hadn't just lost the two mates I had just taken.

Fear burned through me again as I pulled Charlie up, feeling for his pulse. His heart still beat, faint but strong.

Fuck.

I held him in my arms, watching as Mich and Lora knelt over Jaehan. I couldn't make out what everyone was saying, only the dark hum of magic gone wrong.

I looked around, my eyes moving to the door.

Everyone was in here now, our entire group.

Where was the rest of the office then?

Wouldn't an event like this attract others?

"We need to go," I whispered, the sense of dread becoming stronger.

I shook my head, trying to get a hold on all of my dark thoughts. On the panic and terror that wanted to overpower me.

I couldn't let myself think about my mates right now. I had to think about everything else.

"We need to go," I snapped again, this time commanding attention.

Everyone looked at me, and Inferna's eyes widened.

The silence was too absolute.

Too still.

"Portal," she whispered, snapping her fingers a few times. "Portal. Now. For fuck's sake, witches!"

"On it," Alex snarled, rising to his feet.

He started to raise his hands but the building moaned, the floor rumbling beneath us.

I was thrown to the side, Charlie moving with me as the world seemed to tilt. The room was lit up with purple light, streaks that cut the ground into three parts— separating all of us.

Fuck.

I tried to get to my feet but just ended up rolling more. For a split second, it looked like the entire building was coming apart, and then I smelled it.

The taste of dark magic.

The kind that snuffed out cities, the kind that destroyed creatures to dust.

The kind that we called a myth. A legend.

I heard a voice screaming above the roar of brick and wood crumbling.

Get out! GET OUT!

Alex. screaming at the top of his lungs.

My heart felt like it was torn in two. Only Charlie was with me, but I still drew a portal of darkness.

I looked back around the room again, my eyes widening as I stole a glimpse. There was a dark figure that had emerged in the center of the room and it was facing Alex—whose gloves had come off and was giving it lightning.

Fuck.

The darkness seemed to turn, a figure that moved all on its own. I felt my heart skip a beat, another wave of terror overcoming me.

You're coming with me.

Fuck.

I turned, trying to reach for Charlie and push him into the portal I had just made. I managed to give him a shove just as I felt something grip my ankle and yank me back.

I watched my mate fall through just as darkness consumed me.

CHAPTER SEVENTEEN

curses

CHARLIE

I STOOD IN A FOREST, the trees stretching over me as light filtered through the tops. It was golden, its touch pure as it warmed my body.

I was a monster, but it was moments like this where I felt at peace with myself. I didn't have to worry about the men seeing me. I didn't have to worry about being hunted into the dark.

I was here for a reason. I was here for the witch.

They would help me. They would help me find a way to stay out of sight. I didn't have natural camouflage like other creatures. I was pale and bright, like crushed precious stones. There was no way I could hide.

When I first came here, I hadn't anticipated how difficult it would be to understand the world around me. I hadn't realized that never returning home would leave me feeling empty.

I had come from a court of creatures who were part

Cecaelia and part demon. Monsters who could be on land or in the sea. I preferred the land to the water, even though my tentacles helped me more there than here.

I basked in the sunshine for a moment, only to have it disrupted by the sound of rustling.

"*Creature,*" a voice said. "*Why are you in my forest?*"

I looked up, meeting the golden gaze of a woman. She was standing in the shadows, watching me with a piercing curiosity.

"*I seek you, witch,*" I said. "*I come here to beg you to lend me your magic. To allow me to not be seen by the world. I am too bright, and I attract mankind. They fear me, hate me. I am too bright for the darkness, and it has led to me always running.*"

The witch shook her head. "*You are meant for the sea.*"

"*I am not,*" I said, scowling. "*I am meant for this place. The water has never felt like home. I have seen many wonderful things here, but I can't let them see me. I frighten them.*"

The witch let out a sigh, one of pity. "*Very well then. Come with me and we will see.*"

I DRAGGED IN AIR, sitting straight up. Rain fell on me, drenching me in its cold.

For a moment, I wasn't sure who I was. I wasn't sure where I was.

But then I felt the bonds.

Fuck.

FUCK.

I wiped my mouth with one of my tentacles, smearing away the black blood that I had thrown up. I remembered everything now.

Billy. Jaehan.

The office.

Fuck.

I looked around me and realized I was in front of Billy's house. I rolled to my feet, catching myself before I fell straight back onto his lawn.

Lightning crackled up above, the September storm growing stronger. My body trembled as I made my way up to his house.

One of my tentacles reached up, curling around the doorknob. I froze, a shiver working up my spine.

They can see you.

That voice.

I spun around, only to stumble back as fear washed through me.

The witch stood in front of me after all this time. The rain began to pour harder, drenching her. She grinned, flashing fangs.

"*You,*" I whispered. "*Where are my mates?*"

"*Mates?*" She asked, cocking her head. "*Who would ever mate with you? You're a monster. You have no mates.*"

"*I do!*" I yelled, trying to yank the front door of the house open.

I had to get away.

"*Oh you mean these two?*"

I looked back over my shoulder, my eyes widening as both Billy and Jaehan appeared. They both glared at me with hatred and disgust.

Pain and fear curled through me. Why were they looking at me like that?

"*You're disgusting,*" Billy said. "*And that's coming from a demon like me. Your tentacles, you. Everything about you is a turn off.*"

"*I would never be with a being like you,*" Jaehan said, scoffing. "*I'm an omega. Omegas deserve the best, and you are far from that.*"

"Stop," I whispered, but it was almost a beg.

"You wanted them to see you. You wanted the world to see you. Well, now they can ," the Witch cackled. "You're hideous. Ugly. A monster."

I closed my eyes for a moment, the pain and fear becoming stronger. I had worried that they would hate me but they had mated me. They said they loved me and...

I frowned, my heart hammering in my chest.

They did love me.

I opened my eyes again, looking straight at the witch. I looked past them, at the world around us.

All of it had a hue, one that didn't belong. It was like a mirage. A glimmer.

A low growl left me and I let go of the door knob. "Who the fuck are you?"

The witch cocked her head and then her form began to change, morphing until it became a figure of darkness. It was tall and lanky, the energy rolling off it in waves.

Fear. More fear.

I took a steadying breath, mentally strengthening my resolve as the creature continued to grow.

My eyes widened as I recognized what this being was. This god, this creature, this monster— it was one of fear and terror.

It was the ugly one.

It was the monster.

It was the creature without love.

Not me.

"What the fuck are you doing here?" I sneered.

The creature towered over me now. It cocked its head again, tilting it as it looked down at me.

"I take care of the omegas," the creature said, grinning.

Three rows of teeth stared back at me, glinting in the rain.

"I use their fears to keep them locked in their minds, so that they won't know what is happening to them."

"Why?" I whispered, shaking my head.

The thought of this bastard being in Jaehan's mind enraged me.

"Their magic," the creature said. "It's being used."

Why was it telling me this?

"Their magic will set us free."

Fuck. Set what free?

"Your stupid group got in the way though," it hissed. "Breaking what should not be broken. And now you will suffer for it."

"No," I growled. "No. This is my mind. This is my body. Get the fuck out of my head!"

The creature grinned and then snapped its fingers. The world began to wash away like chalk on a sidewalk around us, plunging me into darkness.

I opened my eyes, sitting straight up.

I was back in the office, in the shifting room, and I wasn't alone now.

CHAPTER EIGHTEEN

fear

JAEHAN

"*HOW'S IT GOING?*"

I looked up, smiling as Billy sat down next to me on the bed. He was in his more human form, and wore a simple smile.

"*Good,*" I said, letting out a happy sigh.

"*It's time for us to go,*" he said.

I frowned, my brain feeling heavy with fog. He gave my leg a pat and stood up, yawning as he stretched.

"*Where are we going?*" I asked.

"*What? You don't remember?*" Billy asked, turning around with a frown.

My heart skipped a beat. What was I forgetting?

I looked around the room again, my thoughts slow. We weren't in my apartment, and we weren't at Billy's house. We were...

"*Oh,*" I said, scowling. "*Why are we in my room? At my home?*"

I was sitting in the room I had grown up in. One that had shelves lined with all kinds of books, some in Hangul, others in English. My parents had always let me get whatever books I wanted, and even as I had gotten older, had allowed me to keep my own little personal library here.

I always thought it was their way of making sure I came home sometimes, but I would always come back to visit. Library or not.

"*Your family invited us over, silly,*" Billy said. "*Wanted to be there for us while we mourn.*"

"*Mourn?*" I whispered.

Billy shook his head again, frowning. "*Are you okay? Do you need some coffee maybe? It's like you've forgotten everything...*"

"*I think...yeah. Coffee sounds nice,*" I said.

Billy nodded, heading towards the door. "*I'll be back, human.*"

He left and my quick smile faded, replaced by a frown. Human? Billy had never called me human in that way.

Something felt wrong, but I wasn't sure what it was.

Still, I rolled out of my bed, walking over to my shelves. I dragged my fingers along the book spines, the texture bringing me a little bit of happiness.

I felt a sharp sting and paused, peddling back to one of the books on the shelf.

Only it wasn't a book.

A folder was squeezed between two hard bound spines, sticking out just enough to feel...strange. A soft glow came from it, casting golden light around it. I started to tug it free, but Billy came back into the room, holding a cup of coffee.

"Here you go," he said, smiling.

He came up behind me, reaching around to give me the cup of coffee as he pressed his body to mine.

I let out a little breath, a wave of desire rolling over me but...

It turned into dread.

I felt his breath on my neck, his chuckle reverberating through his chest as his hands fell to my hips.

It was different than any scenario I had lived through, but I recognized the feeling now. The undercurrent of magic that was flowing around me.

I had only known this in one other place.

"You're not Billy," I whispered, my heart pounding in my chest.

The coffee mug in my hands trembled, but I gripped it, feeling a sense of rage.

I spun around, throwing the coffee straight onto what was already turning into a figure of darkness. It hissed, lunging for me right as I dodged it.

Fuck. This was a fucking nightmare.

I felt a tug, one that was new and unfamiliar.

My bonds. My mated bonds.

Fuck.

Think, think, think.

A clawed hand gripped my shoulder, throwing me back across the room. I hit the end of the bed, rolling onto the floor.

"Should have never left us, Jaehan. Should have never run," the creature snarled.

I looked up at it, glaring. "Fuck you. Fuck you for everything. You can't keep us trapped anymore. Whatever your plan is, it won't work."

"It's already working," the creature said, grinning. "Right now, your whole group is facing their fears. Fighting their darkest thoughts. But you and your little omega friends? All of you are having happy little dreams. Ones that will make you create the best magic."

He leaned down his fangs glinting in the light.

"You should have never tried to break my spell, Jaehan. No witch like you could ever overpower a god like me. Your mates are dead and you'll be all alone."

"No," I said, feeling a stab of fear.

I could see it immediately feed him, his words becoming harsher. "They wanted to die anyway. They never wanted to truly be with you. Stuck with a used omega. Who wants that? No one."

"FUCK you," I snarled, kicking out.

I rolled to the side just as he brought his claws down, the wood immediately torn into. I brought my hands together, calling on a spell that would at least knock him over for a moment.

I was loved. I was loved by Billy. By Charlie.

This beast was a liar. He wanted to use my fears against me, to make me believe things that weren't true.

I sent a blast of magic rolling towards him, knocking him back at least a few feet. My heart pounded in my chest as I turned, seeing that glowing book again.

The creature let out a vicious snarl, rolling back to his feet.

I let my instincts guide me and I lunged, gripping the file and ripping it off the shelf.

It fell open, paper flying from it. I stood, letting out a gasp as they swirled down.

The monster snarled, but he was starting to melt.

Everything was starting to melt. To turn into darkness.

I caught one last glimpse of the papers. The words burned at the top, gleaming as if they had been struck through by a highlighter.

```
Horny Resources.
Kim Jaehan- OMEGA.
MAGIC: Yes
MATED: No
MEMORY LOCKED: YES
```

No.

No, my memory wasn't locked anymore.

Everything washed away. I heard a low clicking noise, a weight on my chest.

Hands were shaking me, a very scared and familiar voice saying my name over and over again.

"Jaehan! Please wake up! Jaehan! Jaehan!"

I opened my eyes, meeting the rainbow gaze of my mate.

This was real.

This was no longer a nightmare. No longer a dream or trap.

Tears filled my eyes, blurring my vision.

I let out a noise of surprise as the cat, Biscuit, stood up and jumped off my chest, walking away.

Charlie released a choked noise, dragging me into his arms. He held me tightly and I could feel his heart pounding in his chest.

"Holy shit."

We both looked up, seeing Art sit up. Followed by the others in the room. Inferna, Calen, Cinder, Lora, Mich, Anne, Ember. All of them were slowly waking up, all of our faces wet with tears.

"Fuck. We can see you," Art said, his eyes wide and on Charlie.

Charlie froze and then released a tense breath. I held on to him a little tighter.

"You can see me?" he whispered.

They nodded, eyes widening as they all fell on Charlie.

"Fuck, you're beautiful," Ember said, shaking her head. "And that's saying something since you are definitely not my preference."

I snorted, giving Charlie a gentle squeeze. He shook his head, bewildered.

"You can see all of me?"

"Yes," Inferna said, letting out a long groan. "Fuck. That was some fucked up shit. Is everyone okay? Also, did Biscuit wake everyone else up too?"

A lot of quiet nods, dark gazes locking with each other around the room. Biscuit slinked out of the shifting room, drawing a stressed and tired sigh from Inferna.

"Evil cat," Art muttered.

"Evil? Pretty sure she just helped us," Calen said, shaking his head.

"Where is Billy?" I whispered, my heart squeezing.

"Gone," Charlie said, his voice hoarse. "He and Alex are both gone. Some of the things we thought happened never did. The building never fell apart, I don't think I ever actually threw up blood."

I wrapped my arms around him again, burying my face against his neck.

"I was so scared," I whispered.

"Me too," Charlie murmured, pulling me back to look at me. "I was so scared. It made me believe I was hideous."

Ember snorted from across the room, echoing everyone's opinion.

It made me angry that Charlie ever thought that about himself.

"I know what happened now," Charlie said. "A long time ago I sought out a witch to make me invisible. And she was able to do so, but it came with a cost. I think when Ember did whatever she did, it unlocked a lot of things."

"For all of us," Ember said, shaking her head. "It tried... It tried to make me scared again. To trap me. But I was able to wound it."

"I saw things," I said. "Papers. About me. And I can remember things now. Things about what happened while we were trapped there."

The darkness. The cold darkness, the sounds of people crying. The slow drain of magic from my soul, all feeding a beast.

It wasn't the creature of fear that we needed to worry about.

It was something much worse.

"We have to find Billy," I said, rolling to my feet. "And Alex. Before it's too late."

CHAPTER NINETEEN

monsters

BILLY

I WAS NOT HAVING a good day.

Tomorrow was supposed to be Friday. I was supposed to have the weekend with my newfound mates. I was supposed to be able to clock out and go home.

Instead, my wrists were cuffed and I was chained to a brick wall. One that oozed with some type of liquid. Perhaps it was water, but it smelled like shit, and already my stomach had threatened to empty everything I'd had for breakfast this morning.

I was a demon, therefore I could see in the darkness. But the darkness here was different. It was all encompassing, a shadow that wouldn't disappear.

I heard a grunt to my left and looked up, seeing the outline of Alex. He was hanging from chains like me, his head slumped forward.

"Alex," I hissed. "Alex, wake up. We could really use your lightning fingers right now."

"Alex is battling demons," a dark voice chuckled.

I felt my heart skip a beat, my stomach twisting.

I had been alive for a very very long time. I had known many demons, had fought them and with them. I knew the legends, the myths.

In fact, in a way, I was a legend.

There were monsters.

But then, there were *monsters*.

The sound of scales dragging over the floor made me swallow hard. I focused on the darkness, on the form that slowly stepped forward.

Alfred.

Only, he looked a little different this time.

And this bastard's name was definitely not Alfred.

Gone was the werewolf, replaced by something much nastier. A long serpent's tail with black and green scales curled around his wolven body. His fangs were longer, his fur matted with blood. His claws were long, his eyes burning red.

He was a tall fucker. Nine feet, his shoulders wide.

He parted his jaws, flames glimmering in his throat.

"Aamon," I whispered.

Fuck.

What the fuck was an ancient demon like him doing here?

"Yes," he chuckled, moving forward. "The one and only."

"What are you doing here?" I asked. "You've never involved yourself with the world of humans."

"Of course I have," he said, still creeping closer. He stopped a couple of feet in front of me. "It's the way our world is now. Even ancient demons like myself like to play with mortals. We like to have our empires, such as this company."

I shook my head, feeling a shred of fear.

This wasn't good news. In fact, this was terrible news.

I had never met this demon in the flesh because I had been wise enough to stay away. I had kept out of his way, avoiding being contracted into his legions of demons.

"Aamon," I said. "I don't understand—"

"You can call me Alfred," he corrected. "I like my new name. I like my new life. And I certainly like the magic these little witches can give."

He moved over to Alex, stepping up to the witch. He reached out, taking his head in his claws. He chuckled, his fangs glinting.

"Such magic makes me more powerful than ever. To think that this witch thought he was doing a good thing when he powered me. What a fucking fool."

Fuck.

Alex had summoned him.

FUCK.

"He had no idea," Alfred murmured. "No idea all the pain and suffering he would cause."

The bastard had left out all of this information. Again.

Fucking hell, if we made it out alive, Inferna would hang him by his balls.

"He thought we were friends," Alfred said softly, his voice a low growl. "I loved him. He never loved me. And so I bided my time. And now here we are. All of the omegas have fallen to me, and I've used their magic to grow stronger. And Alex here will be my final sacrifice. The first omega should be the final one, right?"

"You're just hurting creatures like you," I said, my voice dropping into a low sneer. "Why would you do that?"

Alfred looked over at me, embers leaving his tongue as he spoke. "You think I care about other creatures? I command them. Rule them. For thousands of years, I have commanded millions of demons like you. You think you're so strong, Billy, but you are nothing compared to me. Nothing. Try controlling gods of darkness, and then talk to me about caring about little creatures like your friends. They're just part of the food chain. But of course, you know how it goes. You're just pretending."

He let go of Alex and leaned in, his snout only an inch from my face.

"You know, better than anyone, how pointless the lives of these creatures are. You were cut from the same cloth as me, and yet...you choose to work as a nobody. In an office of monsters who are trying to fit into a world they could easily destroy. It takes you two seconds to slaughter a mortal, and yet you are conforming to their ways. From your stupid HR departments to security to taxes and banks. You live paycheck to paycheck, paying rent on a little house in a little neighborhood that you could burn to ashes. You drive a car and make payments, one that can't even fit your full demon form. And you hide like a scared little rat. Tell me, Billy. Who is it that is hurting others? Is it you, a wolf in sheep's clothing, or is it me— someone that is liberating them?"

"How are you liberating them?" I snarled. "Fucking how?"

"By putting their gifts to use," he said. "These omega witches. Their magic is strong. Stronger than even some of the most powerful witches, ones that could rival even me. And yet they throw it away, just like you throw away your gifts."

Alfred leaned in closer, his breath smelling like sulphur.

"They are a waste," he whispered. "Just like your mate is a waste. Jaehan. So much untapped power. You know, when he was trapped in his dreams, he gave my demons one hell of a fight. Killed at least three of them. It's like they forget."

"Forget what?" I growled, yanking against the chains.

"Forget that they are monsters," he breathed, drawing back. "But no worries, little Billy. They will come for you. For Alex. And I will destroy all of them."

"I just don't understand what you're getting out of this," I said, watching as his hideous form moved back towards the darkness.

"Power," he said. "Redemption. Revenge. Alex could have loved me. He could have been mine. But he refused, and now his soul will be mine. But first, I'm going to crush everything he's ever built in his life. Starting with this company. I'm going to burn it to the ground."

I grimaced, watching as he disappeared into a portal. A doorway of darkness.

I let out a breath, closing my eyes for a moment as I registered everything.

All of it made a lot more sense now.

I heard a quiet gasp, the jingle of chains.

My eyes flew open and I looked at Alex, glaring. "Rise and shine, demon summoner. You're officially the world's worst boss."

Alex let out a heavy groan, looking around. "Fuck. What the fuck is happening?"

"Your highschool sweetheart chained us up and told me about his revenge plot on you since you're not gonna be his boyfriend," I said. "And now, everyone I love is going to die and our office is going to be wiped out."

Alex made a noise, squinting. "Fucking hell. God damn it."

"Yeah, bud, I don't think god damned us. I think you did."

Alex looked over at me. "You think I wanted this?"

"No. But you know what? I think you could have told Inferna and crew that you SUMMONED this bastard. That he was not a werewolf, but in fact an ancient demon that commands legions of demons. LEGIONS, Alex. What the fuck were you thinking?"

"I didn't know," he whispered. "I was young at the time. Trying to prove myself. I summoned him and...we became friends."

"Not friends. He was using you. You can't be friends with a demon like that. There are monsters, and then there are evil bastards that should actually stay in hell that don't deserve a little picket fence life. Alfred is one of them. He will do everything in his power to hurt us. To hurt you."

"I know," he rasped. "Fuck. I know. I don't know what to do."

"We need to get out of here. And we need to figure out how to buy some time. Like a couple of months of time. Enough that we can figure out a binding spell for him, one that all of the omegas can cast. With their supposed power, perhaps it would be enough to stop him. And hell, I want a fucking raise. I want a fucking raise and a bonus that will make my cock hard from how big it is."

Alex scoffed, but he didn't disagree.

"And I need you to swear to me that you will not lie anymore, Alex. This cost us."

Alex hesitated for a moment, a shadow falling over his face. "I've fucked up."

"Yes. We all have our dumbass phases. If you survive,

perhaps you'll make it out of yours. Alex, I want a binding promise to me. Now."

Alex ground his teeth, yanking on the chains. He let out a little snarl. "Fuck. Fine."

"I'm a demon and I still don't get why you've lied so much."

"Trying to protect everyone," Alex said.

"No," I said, glaring. "No, that's another lie. Another fucking lie. You were trying to protect yourself. And maybe you were trying to protect him."

He was silent for a moment, his body relaxing. "I think I could have loved him, but he was never meant to be my mate. I never felt the bond to him. I never felt the pull. And I never thought it would be a problem, but then it all changed. And he's been growing in power ever since."

"Right," I said. "Omega. You need your mates. The real ones."

"Yeah," Alex whispered. "As if I will ever find them. I've been waiting. Hoping. You know what a heat is like without your mate? It's torture. Nothing satisfies you. All of the omegas in this office are young, so their suffering was at least somewhat brief. But me? I've been an unmated omega for a very long time now, and every cycle, I lose myself to suffering that can't compare."

"You'll find them one day," I said.

"Now you're lying," Alex whispered.

"No," I said, "I'm not. I didn't think I would find anyone who could love me. I never believed that I would have a mate. Let alone two. But here I am. I came to work this Monday, met Charlie and Jaehan, and I'm here today— a mated demon. A mated monster. To two amazing creatures who I will spend the rest of my life giving all of my love to.

You will get your turn Alex. But first, we need to get the fuck out of this prison."

"I think we're in the basement of the building across from Warts & Claws," Alex said. "He will know if we escape."

"Right," I said, my stomach twisting. "Fuck. Alright. I think I have a plan. But we're going to need a spell, one that is strong enough to give us the time we need."

CHAPTER TWENTY

poppins

CHARLIE

OUR GROUP STOOD in the conference room surrounding a giant white board that Anne was writing on as Inferna gave instructions. Our boss paced back and forth, an evil naked cat in her arms as her red tail swished behind her.

"We know they're close," Jaehan said. "They have to be. It would make sense."

"It would," Cinder said. "Maybe Lora can try to reach out to Billy?"

"I already tried," Lora sighed, leaning against them. "It's no use. Wherever they have him, I can't seem to find him."

"Hmm." Mich and Art both hummed at the same time.

Calen frowned. "What about Alex?"

"What about him?" Inferna asked.

"What if we tried to reach him," Calen said.

"I also tried," Lora said. "No use."

"What if a witch tried to reach him?" Calen asked.

We were all quiet for a moment and Ember cleared her throat. "I could try."

"NO," Inferna, Cinder, Art, and Mich all said at the same time.

"No offense, hun, but after what just happened— I don't think that would be wise. I don't want to deal with that fear demon again," Inferna said, her eyes darkening.

Calen reached out, grabbing her hand for a moment. She gave it a gentle squeeze, giving him a soft but still wicked smile.

Anne sighed, tapping the end of the marker on the board for a moment. "Jaehan," she said, turning to look at my mate.

Jaehan was safely wrapped in my tentacles, leaning against me.

"You said you could remember more right?"

"Yes," he said.

"What do you remember about the beast?"

"He was....he wasn't just a werewolf. Something else," Jaehan said, his voice dropping to barely above a whisper. "He was using our magic to grow stronger. Bleeding it from us. He had the tail of a serpent, a wolfish body, and could breathe fire."

Art made a noise, cursing under his breath.

"What?" Inferna asked, whipping around to look at him.

"That's a demon," Art said. "A very old one. I know of him, but I can't recall the name."

Inferna pressed her lips together and then sighed. "I will be back. I'm going to go make a call."

"If you do that, you know they'll show up," Art said.

"Who?" Mich asked.

"No one," Inferna said. "Don't worry about it. We'll pose it as research."

"Sure," Art snorted, watching as she left the room. He and Calen exchanged knowing looks.

"What?" Cinder asked. "Who is she calling?"

"She has an uncle, godfather, something. He owns a coffee shop but apparently he's been around for awhile," Art said, shrugging. "His beard catches on fire sometimes."

"Weird," Anne said, shrugging. "I mean, we all have that uncle."

Calen snorted. "This guy is good. Better to call him than Dante."

Art and Calen both nodded together, a shell shocked look overtaking their expressions for just a moment.

"Who's Dante?" Jaehan asked.

"Her dad," Art said, glancing up as Inferna came back into the room.

"Well," she said, grimacing. "I have good news and bad news."

"What's the bad news?" Ember asked.

"Bad news is that it sounds like we're dealing with a demon named Aamon," Inferna said. "He is a mean motherfucker. And if it's really him, then I don't think we can kill him. He's been around almost as long as some of our family friends."

All of us gave her a little side look. Who was older than this guy?

"Good news?" Anne asked, giving her a hopeful smile.

"My friends are coming to work early," Inferna said. "Meaning, we're about to have a vampire and an orc to help us break into our neighboring building. I have a feeling that's where they are again. There hasn't been any movement over there. As in, when humans walk by it, they naturally give it a wide enough berth as if it's repelling them. That's usually a good indicator that something is going on. And we know that they've been keeping close to the office."

"I think they want us to find them," I said, drawing everyone's attention.

Inferna held my gaze for a moment and then nodded. "I think so too."

"I don't think omegas should go," I said.

I was immediately met with opposition from Jaehan, Calen, and Ember.

"I agree with Charlie," Cinder said, crossing their arms.

Ember turned around, glaring at them. "No. I'm helping with this."

"No, you should really just go home," Cinder said. "And stay out of harm's way."

"You don't have to protect me anymore," she hissed.

Jaehan turned around, glaring up at me. "You aren't doing this alone," he hissed. "I want to help."

"Hold on," Inferna said. "For fuck's sake. The three of you need to stop. You're who they are after."

"Yes," Calen said, glaring. "But that doesn't mean we shouldn't go."

"That's what the blonde chick in horror movies says before she gets eaten," Mich grumbled.

I was about to say something, when all of us paused. The sound of nails on the floor echoed down the hallway.

We all turned, looking up at the doorway.

None other than Poppins was standing there.

I wasn't sure who moved faster— Inferna or Anne— but Inferna made it to the griffin first. In the blink of an eye, the creature was dragged into the room and body slammed down onto the conference table, Inferna standing over him with her heel pressed against his neck, ready to kill.

"Listen," he wheezed. "Please. Listen. Listen."

"Traitor," she hissed. "We went to fucking college together and you fucking betrayed me."

"I had to," he gasped. "Inferna, please. Please, I can explain."

"Inferna," a voice said, an unfamiliar one.

We looked up at the doorway to see a woman, a vampire. She oozed the same raw sexuality that Inferna did. Her platinum blonde hair fell in curls, her lips were painted blood red, and she wore a set of glasses with a cat eye shape.

I arched a brow. All of us looked between her and Inferna.

"Minni," Inferna said. "About fucking time. Where's Lea?"

"Don't know, we didn't come here together. We aren't on the best speaking terms, but we're here for you. Now, let the poor man speak, love, or else he'll die of a heart attack. His little turkey heart is beating so fast," Minni said, flashing her brilliant fangs.

Inferna eased back, still glaring down at Poppins. "Speak."

"I know where he has Billy and Alex," Poppins wheezed. "I can take you there. I can't do this anymore. I was pulled into this thing and then bound to secrecy and ever since then, I've done so much. So much that I regret."

"Why?" Inferna asked, shaking her head. "Why didn't you ask for help? I've been your friend for years, Poppins."

"I was scared," he whispered. "I'm still scared. He will kill me for this. But I have to do it. I have to break free."

Inferna hissed, baring her fangs.

I took a deep breath and let it out, studying the griffin. I had watched him long enough from the corners of the office to know that he was telling the truth.

"He's not lying," I said. "And I think he's the only way we're going to get close. But I still want the omegas to stay here."

"No," Jaehan said, his voice strong. "No. I refuse. You can't make me stay, Charlie."

I looked down at him, holding his gaze. A tear slid down his face and I sighed, wiping the tear away with a tentacle.

"Jaehan," I sighed. "I just want you safe, my love."

"I know," he whispered. "But I have to help. I need to face these demons too."

Fuck.

I didn't like it, but I wasn't going to fight him on it.

"You must be Art and Calen," Minni purred, giving Inferna's mates a once over. "A little cutie and a very handsome witch. Not bad."

Inferna snorted. "Cut it, Minni. We have serious shit going on."

"Oh, I know," she said, looking around the room at us. "This whole office reeks of dark magic."

Inferna nodded. Poppins started to sit back up, only to immediately lie back down on the table when he received a few warning growls.

"Poppins will show us," Inferna said.

I looked back at the griffin, almost feeling sorry for him.

If the demon we were facing truly was Aamon, then he had signed his own death certificate by coming here.

Inferna jumped down off the table and we all turned, looking at the griffin as he slowly sat up. He grimaced, looking around the room.

"They're in the building across the street. Billy and Alex are down in the basements, in a room that he built for the strongest omegas. I think it's to keep magic from going in and out. The door will have to be opened manually. There are about fifteen monsters and witches guarding it, all ready for all of you to show up. Well, most of you," Poppins said.

"We need to get in and out," Art said. "Quick. Free Billy and Alex."

"And then what? How are we going to give ourselves more time?" Lora asked. "What happens after?"

Silence fell over the room. I pulled Jaehan a little closer, wishing I could hide him away.

"After," Inferna said. "After, we clock out and have a nice three day weekend."

CHAPTER TWENTY-ONE

overtime

JAEHAN

I HADN'T REALIZED it was midnight until Charlie and I stepped out onto the sidewalk, the moon burning above. Even with the city lights, it was bright.

Ominous.

I didn't like that this was happening on a full moon.

The planning had been chaotic, but we had managed to work it out. We at least had an idea of what we were up against now.

I knew more than I wanted to. Unlocking my memories had been both good and bad.

The good— I knew everything that had happened to me now.

The bad— I knew everything that had happened to me now.

It pissed me off that this demon thought it was okay to hurt so many. It enraged me that I had been taken for a whole month, and enraged me even more that others had been taken for longer.

It wasn't fair. All of the things that had happened...

A wave of need rushed through me, a reminder that I was still in heat and that every moment I went without my other mate was another moment of torture.

We should have been in bed right now, cuddled up after fucking each other senseless. Not trying to keep each other from dying at the hands of an ancient demon.

"Jaehan," Charlie whispered, one of his tentacles wrapping around my forearm.

His touch soothed me. I knew he could feel my emotions through our mated bond. We were both using the feeling as a lifeline right now, a little flicker of hope that we would save Billy.

Wherever they were keeping him, it was somewhere that blocked the feelings of our bond. It was like running down a dead end road when you swore it kept going— whatever was holding him was a block.

"I love you," Charlie said, giving me a gentle squeeze.

"I love you too," I said, my voice soft.

"We're going to find him. And then we're going to go home and put this nightmare behind us."

I nodded, hoping that was true. I wanted to believe it. I wanted to believe that the three of us were walking out of here tonight.

The two of us crossed the road, heading straight for the alley to the side of the building that we knew held our mate. The idea that he was so close and yet being hidden from us was driving me crazy.

The rest of our group had split up into teams with different purposes.

Charlie and I were going to play as a distraction, to

bring out the witches and monsters that were waiting on us. We would lure them out of the building, where two of the other teams would ambush them.

Meanwhile, Poppins, Inferna, Minni, and Cinder would be going down into the basement.

The decision to split the group up the way it was had been hard. Mates wanted to be with mates and it was difficult to be separated.

All of us were on edge.

I was glad that Charlie was with me, even though we were acting as a distraction.

We went around to the back of the building, creeping along the fence. I peeked around the corner, spotting the access door.

There was someone standing outside of it.

Someone that looked human but most definitely was not.

"There's one," I whispered. "A witch, I think. I'm going to handle them and then if you can get the door open, we can both go in and draw the creatures out."

Charlie nodded. "Assume that they will kill you."

I took a deep breath and then went around the corner, throwing up a blast of magic that put a hole straight through the fence. I heard the witch's shout as he began to speak a spell, running straight for me.

Anger snapped through me and I pulled on the currents of magic running in my blood, on all of the power that I had a glimpse of in my memories.

That demon had wanted me because my power was stronger than I could have ever imagined.

I felt the witch's magic flying towards me like arrows, so I drew up a shield. Words flew from my lips, spells echoing around me as we fought.

I had to be quick.

The two of us collided and I slammed them into the ground, speaking a sleeping spell. They made a noise right before they passed out beneath me, their head rolling to the side.

The hinges on the door creaked and I turned, watching as Charlie used a tentacle to yank it open. I ran to him and we slipped inside.

The building smelled like an office. Like papers and dust.

Heat bloomed in my chest again and I gasped.

The mating bonds to Billy.

Charlie spun around, looking at me with wide eyes for a moment.

"He's close," I whispered.

My mate scowled, his head whipping back to look down the hallway. It was quiet and dark, the only sound aside from our breathing was the AC.

"Come on," Charlie said, moving down the hall.

The two of us moved quickly, staying aware for any signs of other monsters or witches.

I could feel the bond growing stronger and stronger the further into the building we went.

The two of us burst through a set of doors just as a familiar voice screamed. "GET DOWN!"

The two of us hit the floor just as a blast of darkness slammed into the wall right above us. I heard the snarl and hiss of a demon and Charlie's tentacles yanked me to the side, looking up to see a monster unstick from the ceiling and hit the floor.

"Billy," I whispered, looking up at where the attack had come from.

Before Charlie and I could even stand, we were pulled

into the arms of our mate. Tears filled my eyes, a sob escaping me as we held him close. I pulled back for a moment, making sure it was him, before burying my face in his neck and breathing in his scent.

"Fuck," Billy whispered. "Fuck. I knew I felt the two of you. I knew it."

"What happened?" Charlie rasped, looking at Billy with the same worry that I felt.

"A lot," Billy said quickly. "We have to go. We have to get out."

"Billy," a firm voice said. "Come on. All of you."

Alex hovered over the three of us, his face twisted in concern. His fingers were lit up with electricity, his eyes burning as bright as stars.

The three of us got to our feet, moving towards the door, but then they slammed shut.

A snap of fear made me turn around, meeting the eyes of a demon who had caused me so much pain over the last couple of months. So much suffering.

Billy and Charlie took a step in front of me, a low growl rumbling from my mates. Alex let out an uneasy breath.

"You think it'll be that easy?" the demon asked.

All of us were standing in the lobby of the building. The lights were off, the only light coming from the moon and city outside. I looked to my right, seeing the front doors.

Could we make a run for it? If I blasted open the front?

"Alfred," Alex said, his voice cracking with rage. "Let them go. They have nothing to do with what is happening."

"You know that's a lie," Alfred chuckled, cocking his wolven head. "As if I would let any omegas go after you freed so many."

"Let. Them. Go," Alex sneered. "It's not worth it, Alfred. You can keep me."

The demon lifted his lips in a snarl, baring his teeth. "No. In fact, I think I want this omega. Jaehan. You remember me, little one?"

I swallowed hard, my heart skipping a beat. "Yes," I said, glaring. "I do, you fucking bastard."

Alfred chuckled, creeping closer.

Billy and Charlie both stepped in front of me more, blocking me.

"No," I said, trying to squeeze by them. "Don't block me. You'll get hurt."

Charlie hissed at me, his tentacles shoving me back. "You're an idiot if you think we're going to let him touch you."

"Listen to your mate, Charlie boy," Alfred said, his voice booming. "He's a lot smarter than you if you think you could possibly fight me."

None of this was part of the plan, but we had to improvise now.

One of Charlie's tentacles curled around my waist, but I still managed to push between him and Billy.

"Jaehan," Billy snarled.

I ignored him, glancing over at Alex.

He looked down at the ground, his eyes sliding over to me.

When I tell you, I need you to take my hand. I'm going to use your magic, I heard Alex say.

I gave a slight nod, refocusing on the demon.

Alfred really was one scary looking monster.

"I just don't get it," I said, staring him down. "I don't understand why you're doing this."

"Oh, yes you do. You know what I am now. You remember," Alfred said.

He was only a few feet from us now. He parted his jaws, flames curling on his tongue.

"You know what you are too. How different you are. There are only so many omegas in the world, and you all flock to Alex here. Why do you think that is?"

I hadn't thought about that. I didn't really know Alex, had never talked to him aside from when I was rescued and then hired on.

But there was something about him. Standing this close to him, I could feel the hum of his power. It was pulling me closer, a magnet drawing me in.

"I won't kill you," Alfred chuckled.

I stared at him, my muscles tensing.

"Just your mates."

He lunged and I was thrown to the side by a tentacle, slamming straight into Alex as Billy and Charlie collided with Alfred.

I started to roll to my feet but I felt Alex grab my hand, his grip stronger than iron.

"Trust me," he said, looking over at me. "Please."

I held his gaze for a moment and then tore it away, horror washing over me as I looked up to see Billy and Charlie facing the demon.

"Okay," I whispered.

The moment I agreed to trust him was the moment I felt all of my magic leave me. I screamed, my voice louder than it had ever been.

Alfred spun around as all the glass in the lobby shattered, splashing over the floor like sharp raindrops.

Alex never let go of my hand, holding on to me. My vision started to dot and I felt the bonds with Charlie and Billy, knew that they could feel my pain.

I looked up at Alex and my eyes widened as he held up his free hand.

Lightning burst from his fingertips, blinding all of us. I looked away as the air became electric, the smell of fur burning becoming stronger. I heard a fierce scream, one that reminded me of a dying beast.

A wounded monster.

Silence fell over us and Alex let go of my hand, falling back on the floor.

I felt my magic return, flooding me. I gasped, falling to the floor.

Darkness slowly fell over me just as my mates came into view, both screaming my name.

CHAPTER TWENTY-TWO
freaky friday

BILLY

IT HAD BEEN A NIGHTMARE, but all of us were okay.

Both Alex and Jaehan had passed out after using the amount of magic that they did. When the windows and doors in the lobby had shattered, Inferna and the crew had been able to finally come into the building.

All of the monsters and witches they believed to be there had been there, but they had all been dead.

Alfred had sacrificed them to create a protection circle so that he could trap my mates with me.

He had wanted to use Jaehan and Alex together.

I could see why now.

There had been a lot of chaos. Jaehan had remained unconscious for an hour until sitting straight up and nearly giving Charlie a heart attack.

Anne, surprisingly, had been the one to offer to take Alex to her place to help him.

Within a few hours, our group had managed to come to the same conclusion.

Alfred was gone.

We were safe.

For now.

And all of this could resume on Monday.

It was Friday morning, the sun was about to rise. We were off for the day, off for the weekend. We had survived that evil bastard of a demon.

There was a lot to figure out, a lot to talk about, a lot to plan— but I could barely give a damn now that we were home and safe.

This week had been long, especially the last twenty-four hours.

The three of us plopped onto my bed, a series of groans and sighs following.

"This week was hell," Jaehan said, snorting. "Hell and heaven."

"I agree," Charlie chuckled. "And I don't know. I don't know how I like being seen. You know what Inferna told me before we left the office?"

"What?" I asked, even though I had overheard the conversation. A small grin spread across my face.

"She said that I have to wear normal clothes or else she will have Cinder talk to me and it will be a performance issue!"

Jaehan and I both laughed. I turned over onto my side, looking at my two mates.

"We told you," Jaehan said. "Inferna won't tolerate that."

"You try finding a shirt that fits around tentacles coming out of your back," Charlie sighed.

"We'll find you something over the weekend," I said. "Especially if we're still meeting Jaehan's family."

"Yes," he said, relaxing. "My parents will be happy to meet you. They'll be your family too."

Warmth spread through my chest and I leaned over, kissing him on the cheek. He turned, catching my mouth with his own.

I felt a wave of need, his scent washing over me.

A tentacle slid down my body, running over my hardening cocks.

"Fuck," I breathed, drawing back for a moment. "It feels like it's been too long."

"It does," Charlie grunted, stealing a kiss from Jaehan.

I watched them, my cocks now fully hard.

Fuck. I was tired from everything but not tired enough to not enjoy the two of them.

I rolled out of bed, shredding my clothes and then changing into my full form.

Jaehan moaned as Charlie's tentacles began to strip him for us.

I growled and grabbed his clothing, tossing it to the floor. I climbed onto the bed, straddling his thighs.

He let out a helpless moan as Charlie started to tease him. The suckers of his tentacles tugged on Jaehan's nipples, leaving soft marks on his skin as they moved. I reached down and began to stroke his cock, watching as he grew hard between my claws.

Charlie looked up at me and smiled. I leaned down and kissed him, groaning as our tongues met.

Fuck.

I grunted and drew back, gripping his head firmly. "I want you to use your tentacles on our cocks," I said.

Charlie nodded, his head tilting back for a moment as Jaehan leaned up and started to suck one of his nipples.

I felt a tentacle wrap around my cocks, taking over Jaehan's too. The tentacle bound them together and began to move, jerking our shafts together.

Both of us gasped in pleasure, a soft moan leaving me.

"Fuck," I sighed. "Fuck. I need to cum so badly."

"We all do," Charlie groaned. "Fuck, I like how that feels."

Jaehan made little suckling noises as he played with Charlie's nipples.

"Take off your pants, Charlie," I whispered. "Now."

Charlie obeyed, slipping free of the last of this clothing. His cock sprang free, hard and needy. Precum dripped from the tip, the ridges and suckers pulsing.

"Our little omega is still in heat," I said, watching as Jaehan started to move his hips. "Still desperate to be fucked and bred."

"We should breed him together," Charlie said, grunting as pleasure worked through him.

The tentacle let go of our cocks and I moved off him, pushing his legs apart. He let out a desperate noise, his cock standing straight up as I ran my fingers down his ass. I played with him, making sure that he was slick and ready. Making sure that he would be able to take one of my cocks and Charlie's too.

"Lie down," I said, looking at Charlie. "Jaehan, get on top of him."

They both obeyed me. I smiled, watching as Charlie lay out on the bed and Jaehan straddled him.

"Warm him up," I commanded.

Charlie knew exactly what I meant. Two of his tentacles immediately wrapped around his body, while another two moved towards his ass. I reached down and started to stroke one of my cocks as I watched, turned on by seeing our mate take the tentacles.

Jaehan gasped, moaning as the tentacles slid inside of him.

"Fuck," he groaned. "Fuck, Sir. Please."

"Please, what?" I snorted.

"I want you both to fuck me," he gasped.

"So impatient," Charlie teased, moving his tentacles deeper. He began to thrust them in and out, all while wearing a wicked grin. "Such a needy omega."

I smirked. I liked watching Charlie slide into a more dominant role, especially knowing how submissive he had been to me.

"We're going to break your heat," I said, moving closer to him.

He whimpered. Both Charlie and I sucked in a breath, the sound making us harder.

Fuck.

"He needs it," I said, my voice thickening.

I didn't have the patience to tease him too much. I hadn't realized how desperate I was to fill him with my cock, to breed him with Charlie.

I looked past him to my tentacled mate and he winked at me, his fangs gleaming hungrily.

He was just as desperate as I was.

"I can take both of you," Jaehan rasped. "Please. I'm begging you."

Charlie drew in a sharp breath. "I can't wait. I need to be inside of him. My cock is ready to burst."

I nodded, already leaning forward and gripping his hips.

I lifted him as Charlie pulled his tentacles free, lining

up his massive cock. I pressed my lower cock against his, gripping the top one and stroking it.

Jaehan groaned as he slowly lowered himself, taking both of our cocks. Inch by inch.

The three of us groaned in pleasure. I fought for control, fought the urge to plunge straight into my omega mate.

I felt tentacles wrap around my body and looked down, moaning as they wrapped around my muscles.

"Ah fuck," Jaehan gasped. "You're both so big. So fucking big."

"You're doing so good," Charlie said softly. "Taking both of our monster cocks like a good boy."

"We're going to breed you," I snarled, giving a little harder of a thrust.

He cried out, his voice music to my ears.

Finally, both of us were buried completely inside of him. I let out a long growl and leaned forward, kissing his neck as I began to pull my cock out and thrust it back inside of him.

He groaned, making all sorts of little delicious noises.

Charlie cursed under his breath and grabbed Jaehan's hips, starting to move him up and down on our cocks. We found a rhythm, one that had me thrusting harder and harder.

"I'm going to cum," Jaehan gasped.

"Do it," I said. "I want you to cum on Charlie while we're inside of you."

Charlie just made a moan. The two of us rutted into our mate harder, listening to his breaths become pants until he cried out. His cum shot out onto Charlie's chest, his lungs heaving as he caught his breath.

I shoved him forward, pushing his face down into his cum. "Lick it up," I growled.

He began to lick it up, squeaking as I buried my cock inside of him over and over. I could feel the ridges of Charlie's cock rubbing against mine as we took him in tandem, the feeling driving me crazy.

"I'm getting close," Charlie huffed.

"Me too," I moaned. "Me too."

Jaehan licked up the last of his cum and collapsed on Charlie's chest as we fucked him, making soft moans.

"Together," I grunted. "Cum together."

Charlie nodded, still gripping our mate's hips.

"Now," I gasped, slamming all the way inside of him.

We both groaned together and I started to cum, filling up Jaehan at the same moment that Charlie did.

I stilled, catching my breath as I emptied the last of my seed inside of him.

Charlie and Jaehan both let out soft little moans, more tentacles wrapping around us.

Jaehan lifted his head slowly. "I think...I think my heat is broken."

"Oh yeah?" I said, grinning.

I kissed his back, letting out a happy sigh.

"Yeah," he said, collapsing back on Charlie.

Charlie smiled, stroking his body in gentle rubs.

"I'm going to pull out," I said.

Jaehan and Charlie both nodded and I was quick, pulling my cock free and grabbing a towel from the door. I tossed it to Charlie and he caught it, flipping Jaehan onto it and then pulling out.

I smiled, plopping down on the edge of the bed.

I was happy.

Happier than I had ever been.

"I love you," I said, looking at both of them. "Both of you. So much."

"I love you too," Charlie said, giving me a gentle smile.

"I love you both," Jaehan said sleepily, relaxing into the bed. "I think I could sleep a million years."

"For once, I think I could too," I said, watching as his eyes closed. "And we've got a three day weekend."

"I propose a shower, food, and then sleep—"

A soft snore left Jaehan, making both of us grin.

"Well," Charlie said, leaning back on the bed. "Sleep, shower, and then food?"

"Yes," I said. "And then a glorious weekend with my mates."

"One where we can forget about work. And about the fact that I need a shirt."

"And the fact that Monday will be here before we know it," I said, climbing onto the bed on the other side of Jaehan.

The three of us curled up and I turned over, watching as the sun started to rise through the blinds.

This week has been hell, but It had been worth it.

I was a monster, a creature of darkness, but I had found love.

I had found both of my mates.

A happy smile slowly spread over my lips and I closed all six of my eyes, pushing away every worried thought.

Monday, a new battle could come, but it was Friday and we were officially off the clock.

horn-y resources

ALFRED- HEAD OF HR

ALEX THOUGHT that he had won.

He truly thought his little magic trick had been enough to send me back to hell.

It hadn't sent me back to hell, but it had wounded me. Just enough to make me take a seat and think about plans.

"Sir," a voice said.

I looked up to see my agent. My most trusted one.

She had been with since the beginning. She knew about Alex. She knew why I did what I did.

Hell, she had been the one to slaughter all of the monsters and witches in the building earlier.

Their sacrifice had been necessary and neither one of us had flinched. All of them were pawns at the end of the day.

Well, almost all.

She wasn't as powerful as me, but I didn't use her as a pawn.

I used her as a queen.

"I think it's time," she said, leaning against the doorway of my office.

This office was one I hadn't been in for years, but it had still been well kept.

"While you heal," she said, "I will take care of this. I will bring them to you. Whomever you want, sir."

"I want an omega," I said. "I need one to feed. To heal."

"Which one, sir?" she asked, baring sharp fangs.

"Bring me the one who unlocked all of their memories. The one who we should have taken long ago. She thinks that she is safe, but she isn't. And I want her power. She's the only omega aside from Alex who understands what she can do."

"Yes, sir," she said. "I will bring her to you. What is her name again?"

"Ember."

clio's creatures

Hello Creatures!

My name is Clio Evans and I am so excited to introduce myself to you! I'm a lover of all things that go bump in the night, fancy peens, coffee, and chocolate.

IF you had the chance to be matched with a monster- what kind would you choose?!

Let me know by joining me on FB and Instagram. I'm a sucker for werewolves to this day.

P.S.

Join my Newsletter by clicking here- I won't spam you, but I will offer you fun rewards for being one of my monster loving creatures.

Clio's Creature Newsletter

also by clio evans

CREATURE CAFE SERIES

Little Slice of Hell

Little Sip of Sin

Little Lick of Lust

Little Shock of Hate

Little Piece of Sass

Little Song of Pain

Little Taste of Need

Little Risk of Fall

Little Wings of Fate

Little Souls of Fire

Little Kiss of Snow: A Creature Cafe Christmas Anthology

WARTS & CLAWS INC. SERIES

Not So Kind Regards

Not So Best Wishes

Not So Thanks in Advance

Not So Yours Truly

Not So Much Appreciated

Made in the USA
Middletown, DE
31 October 2022

13828125R00104